Ivy

Tale of a Homeless Girl
in San Francisco

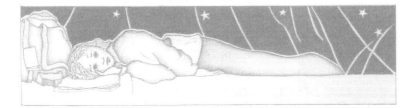

OTHER BOOKS BY SUMMER BRENNER

POETRY

Everyone Came Dressed as Water
From the Heart to the Center

FICTION

The Soft Room
Dancers and the Dance
One Minute Movies
Presque nulle part

IVY

*Tale of a Homeless Girl
in San Francisco*

SUMMER BRENNER

Illustrated by
MARILYN BOGERD

CREATIVE ARTS BOOK COMPANY
Berkeley • California • 2000

The drawing for chapter 18 was especially commissioned
from Manon Bogerd-Wada, age 12.

Ivy is published by Donald S. Ellis
and distributed by Creative Arts Book Company.

For information contact:
Creative Arts Book Company
833 Bancroft Way
Berkeley, California 94710

ISBN 0-88739-287-3
Library of Congress Catalog Number 002-102006

Printed in the United States of America

*To my dear daughter, Joanna,
and to her friends, Hannah and Mariel,
whose childhoods we shared*

ACKNOWLEDGMENTS

The author would like to express her appreciation for the efforts of all those working on behalf of the homeless, especially the volunteers at the Drop-In Center in Berkeley, where women and children can find shelter during the day. Also, great thanks to Michael Weber and John Bean for their inspiration, and son Felix for his unwavering support.

Table of Contents

IVY

Tale of a Homeless Girl
in San Francisco

Chapter 1

I T WAS A FEBRUARY DAWN, AND THE SKY WAS A CLEAR PINK, GLAZED and shiny like a crystal chandelier. Streaks of yellow streamed through the sky, looping like ribbons in the wind while the clouds reflected like lilies in the water. Although the colors of the morning looked as if the air ought to be hot, it was quite chilly, unusually cold in fact, and a light layer of gossamer frost lay across everything.

Small fishing boats, returning from a long night at sea, skimmed across the pink reflection of the clouds, passing silently towards their berth, their home in the docks at the far end of San Francisco Bay.

Ivy watched them from inside her sleeping bag, placed at the edge of the water. She peeked over her covers and studied the sky's reflection in the water and the boats returning home. She wondered when she would have a house again to skim home to, like the boats bumping across the small waves of the bay.

"Everything looks as if it belongs somewhere," she sighed aloud. "Everything looks as if it has a place."

As far as she could tell, the trees appeared planted in the right spots. The squawking bluejays who flitted between the high branches acted if they rightfully belonged in them. The ants that crawled in long, straight lines by her side, looked confident of where they were going, where they had been. All the creatures had a place, but she and her father had almost nothing. They were homeless.

Ivy and Poppy — for that was what she called her father — had been homeless for almost three months. Before that they had lived in a loft in downtown San Francisco. A loft was not a house, not an apartment, not a flat, but it was their home. Indeed, it was a grand place to live with so much space that Ivy could roller skate in the living room, while Poppy painted his strange paintings in the area called his studio. They had hung a hammock and a swing from the high rafters and planted a vegetable garden on the roof in the middle of the city.

Poppy didn't own the loft. He rented it, and so when they first moved in, it was necessary to ask permission from his landlord to change it.

"I'll pay for the supplies and renovations myself," he offered.

"Yes," the landlord agreed, and Poppy went to work.

There they lived in the loft for five years, and Ivy had just turned twelve years old when they were evicted. It was in November that two men appeared in their doorway to carry off all their belongings — their beds, tables, chairs, the radio and record player, their clothes, books, rugs, appliances, and kitchenware. These were to be placed in storage until Poppy had enough money to pay the back rent and the storage charges.

Fat chance! There wasn't even money to buy food and no one to turn to for help. Poppy's few friends were almost as poor as they were. Ivy's mother had died when she was three, and her family in Australia was too far away. Poppy had no brothers, no sisters, and his father had long ago disowned him. Ivy had never met her grandfather, although from time to time she heard about his wealth, his houses, his position of importance. She didn't know why Poppy and his father had such strong disagreements, but whenever she asked, she was told it was too complicated for a child to understand.

Ivy knew that meant it was too complicated for Poppy, not for her. Whenever he chose not to discuss something, she had learned that it was painful for him and had little to do with her. After all, in her twelve years she had already learned many things. She knew how to read quite well and work with numbers. Poppy had taught her to strum his battered old mandolin and to sing songs. Tall for her age and exceedingly strong, she had beaten every boy in her class in arm wrestling. Her arms and legs were muscular, her skin freckled and pale, her eyes the green color of a crocodile pool which looked directly out at everything with a fierce, piercing gaze. She could devise the best places to hide money and the facial expressions to show that she didn't have a dime. She knew how to find her way through the city. She knew how to use the catalogs in the library. She knew where the homeless shelters were. She knew how to draw and paint and was always the best artist as well as the best arm-wrestler in her class.

Her most distinguished and unattractive features were her thick, tangled honey-colored hair which hung to her waist and a red birthmark on her left cheek in the shape of a star.

"That's where the angels kissed you," her father said about the wine-colored star. "The angels always mix a tiny bit of imperfection with the perfect parts — like a dash of salt in a sugar cake."

Still Ivy hated her birthmark and the tangles in her hair. Hated her board-flat chest, hated that her mother had died, hated her grandfather for hating Poppy, and now hated their homeless, difficult life.

In fact, during these homeless, forlorn weeks and months, not much of what Ivy knew, nor much of what she had learned, counted. The only thing that really mattered at all was for her and Poppy to have a home again.

Ivy stared at the fishing boats from her sleeping bag. The sailors on deck were bundled in warm, woolly caps and coats. Their hands were covered with thick gloves, and from a distance they looked friendly.

Ivy had discovered that almost everyone looked friendly from a distance, but when she got up close to a person, she had to be able to read them like a book. There were crazy people as kind as lambs and sane people as mean as rabid dogs. From a distance it might not be possible to tell the difference, but if you were homeless and lived on the streets, you had to know.

Glancing over at her father, Ivy called softly, "Poppy."

Poppy turned over in his sleeping bag and answered her with a tiny snore. His hair, curly and honey-colored like his daughter's, stuck out in all directions from his head. His unshaven beard was short and redder than the hair on his head. His complexion was tanned and wrinkled from living outdoors. He pulled his sweater over his eyes to block out the light from the rising sun.

It would be another few minutes before he awoke, and to amuse herself, Ivy folded her fingers into a telescope shape and held her eye against the ring of her thumb and finger, watching the distant boats as if they were on a miniature stage, performing a tiny play for her amusement. She imagined that one of the boats had come from an island called Pago Pago and that silver dolphins had followed it in the starlight. The captain of that boat could speak to the dolphins, and from them he had learned the secrets of life.

"Silver dolphin," she could almost hear the captain say, "tell me a secret of the sea."

To which the dolphin replied,

> *Before there was land*
> *there was only sea*
> *and the creatures*
> *the whale, the porpoise, and me*
> *walked on the sand*
> *and our legs were free.*

Although Ivy laughed at her rhyme, at that moment, it was no joke that she was cold. Her knees and ankles were stiff from sleeping on a hard, rocky place. Her back and shoulders ached, and her mouth tasted like a soggy mushroom.

She wriggled her arms, fingers, and hands. She unlocked her legs and knees. She arched her toes towards the bridge and the frosty bay, towards the faraway, tropical island of Pago Pago, thousands of miles to the west. She turned her neck and stretched it south. That was the direction where she and Poppy would be heading for breakfast, over to the homeless shelter off Market Street. If they missed the hot breakfast, they could usually grab cold cereal and milk. Ivy's stomach rumbled with hunger.

"It won't be long," she said, patting her stomach affectionately. Then she touched the birthmark on her cheek which rose slightly from her skin. Her green eyes widened up at the pink silky sky. Its beauty made her ache with a sadness that was partly the simple beauty of the sky, partly the heavy feeling in her heart — the sadness of feeling so alone and knowing how alone Poppy felt too, the sadness of watching the boats coming from somewhere and going somewhere else. Her entire body was filled with discomfort. The night had been cold and the ground hard.

When Ivy was little, it was different. They often slept outdoors, and she loved lying close to the ground under the stars. That was camping. That was before they came to San Francisco, before they fixed up the loft, before they were homeless. The two of them had traveled around the West. Poppy painted paintings and tried to sell them as they went along. If nobody wanted to buy a painting, he worked at odd jobs — mending people's roofs or fences, fixing sinks and garbage disposals, building cabinets and constructing decks. Often he would trade his skills, exchanging work for food or a place to stay. If they got into a pinch, he would offer up his services, for he could do almost anything when it came to homebuilding. He could work as a carpenter, plumber, painter, plasterer, mason, or electrician.

Apparently, Poppy was a clever man, and for most of Ivy's life, things had gone along. They weren't rich, but there was enough. Poppy said that their health and freedom would suffice as riches for him. He said money turned even rich men into slaves. That's what had happened to his father, and he was determined not to let it happen to him.

When Ivy was six years old, Poppy decided to settle down in one place. Out of the blue, he said it was time for her to go to real school. "Instead of the school of life," he added with his shy laugh.

He showed Ivy the photos of San Francisco — the beautiful bridges and the great Bay; the dramatic, slippery hills with apartment houses and hotels perched on their peaks; and the cable cars that traveled up and down the steep grades. He asked if she would like to live there. "I think you'll like it," Poppy said.

A spring of tears rushed from the pit of Ivy's stomach up her throat to her eyes. "I don't know if I'll like it," she answered tentatively, rubbing the birthmark on her cheek, "but I'll try."

"That's the best part about you, princess. You are willing to try."

Before Poppy found their loft, they lived cozily in an old red van, parked along the rugged Pacific coast. Ivy was little and didn't think it was strange that they lived their life like campers. She went along with everything, and Poppy was proud to say that in those years she had never been hungry.

"Once this red van was a sailboat," Poppy told her, "until it wandered onto shore. There it found four wheels, traded its barnacled keel for an axle, so it could take us around and find out about life on land." While he spoke, Poppy patted the van's dashboard as if it were alive. "If it hadn't been for me, this old thing would have stayed lonely and rusty in the sea." He pointed to his trusty brain, as if to say that he could figure anything out.

Ivy loved her father's stories. When he put her inside them, she believed that was where she really lived. She was always warm inside his words, always filled with enough to eat.

She couldn't say when things began to change. First, Poppy hadn't been able to sell his paintings. Then, he couldn't find work as a handyman. Nobody seemed to need his services as a carpenter, plumber, electrician, mason, or painter. He said if he had had a contractor's license, it would have been different, but suddenly there was no work for him.

When they were evicted from the loft, it wasn't easy to believe that anything would be right again. Not even his funny stories could reassure her.

The shivers in Ivy's body started to melt in the sliver of sun. The fishing boats and cotton clouds passed out of view. The pink shades of dawn shifted to pale, icy blue. Her stomach's rumbling ceased, but a sadness even worse than hunger still persisted.

Ivy said to herself, "Surely it could have been simpler for me. Surely an angel in the universe could have made it easier for Ivy Elizabeth Katherine Bly."

Chapter 2

WHILE POPPY SLEPT, IVY CRAWLED OUT OF HER SLEEPING bag. HER eyes roamed up and down the tall eucalyptus trees above her. The leaves of the trees were dusty grey green, and a large seagull soared over their branches. Ivy could hear the bird but couldn't see it, for the trees were close and thick. Strips of bark peeled off the trunks and lay on the ground like a tattered carpet.

Several yards up the hill above the harbor, a round and glistening thing caught her eye. In the light of the rising sun, it threw its surface back like a tiny prism.

After a moment, the thing blinked and a small piece of landscape moved. Now Ivy saw that it was the eye of a small animal, lying completely still, so still someone might think it had died.

Ivy's eye stared straight at the animal's eye. Around that bright glinting orb lay a soft patch of white, and around that patch extended a head of dark fur. The animal had spots all over its body. Its ears were floppy, and its wet nose looked as it had been dipped in black ink. Its paws were large like a puppy's. There was a streak of slobber around its snout. No doubt about it — it was a dog.

As Ivy raised one knee up to take a step, the dog's hind leg twitched in response. She smiled, and the dog opened its mouth in a toothy grin. Some dribble from its tongue fell onto the ground. Suddenly a tail came into view, whipping back and forth like the branch of a strong wind. Back and forth, back and forth it wagged across the dirt.

Ivy started walking carefully uphill. The dog studied her with amusement and caution. Just as she reached down to pet the furry, fluffy head, an angry voice barked loudly behind her.

"Ivy, get away from that animal! Get away — right now!"

Both dog and girl stiffened. The dog's tail stopped wagging, and Ivy's smile vanished.

"Ivy, do you hear me?" Poppy shouted as he crawled out of his sleeping bag. In an instant, he was by her side. He grabbed her hand and yanked her back towards their little campsite.

"Don't you know that dog could be sick?" He asked angrily. "Don't you realize that it could bite you to bits?" It was anger that Poppy used to cover up his fear.

Ivy looked up at the spotted pup, which was rolling happily in the dirt and leaves, arching its spine like a cat.

"I don't think he is sick," Ivy reasoned. "I don't think he's mean either. I think he would probably like to get to know us."

"I don't care what you think," Poppy snapped. "You don't know anything about dogs."

Now Ivy was angry and dismayed. How could Poppy accuse her of not knowing anything about dogs?

"I mean you don't know anything about that particular dog," he continued, his eyes softening, his fury drifting away like the pink clouds in the sky. "That's what I meant to say, princess."

Ivy didn't have to ask what made her father angry. Recently a girl at a homeless shelter had been chewed in the face by a stray dog.

Meanwhile up the hill, the dog opened its mouth, yawned, and then collapsed back on its hind legs, wagging its tail once again.

"See," Ivy said, pointing at the creature. "He wants to be our friend."

Poppy smiled at the sight of the animal wiggling in pure friend-
liness. "Cute," Poppy admitted and beckoned to the dog with his
hand who instantly slithered on its legs towards them, wagging and
drooling.

Ivy ventured her opinion again, "It doesn't seem mean. It does-
n't seem sick."

True, the dog had a careless, trusting air. Its coat was shiny, its
gaze clear. There was no crust around its eyes or snout, and its nails
were clipped.

Poppy rummaged in his tin box and pulled out several bits of
bread. He gave one to Ivy to munch. Then he threw a second in
the air where the dog caught it like a frisbee.

"You cannot have a dog," Poppy said sternly, reading his daughter's mind. "You understand that, don't you, Ivy?" He paused to pull
his fingers through her tangled honey-colored locks. "I wish you
could, but you can't. Is that understood?"

Ivy nodded.

There was hardly the means to feed themselves. They certainly couldn't afford to feed a dog. Also, dogs were prohibited at the
homeless shelters where they usually took their meals. It was difficult enough for the two of them — hard to find a decent place to
eat, almost impossible to find a safe place to sleep. The nicest
homeless centers were reserved for women with children, and shelters for men were places Poppy hated to go. They often accommo-
dated those who were rowdy, drunk, crazy, or drugged. Sometimes
these men said nasty things about Ivy's pretty hair. Or asked Poppy
if Ivy was his girlfriend. These questions infuriated Poppy and
embarrassed Ivy. That's why it was preferable to sleep outdoors,
despite the cold weather.

"I'm in a big hurry this morning," Poppy said. "I don't have
time to discuss dogs."

Ivy pushed back a tear. There was no use in arguing or protest-
ing.

"I wish you could have a dog, but you can't," Poppy repeated
with a note of regret.

Ivy turned away from Poppy, away from the dog. She knew
what she had to do next and there was no sense making a fuss. She

vigorously shook her sleeping bag to oust any bugs, then smoothed and rolled it into a ball, and tied it with a piece of string. Next, she filled a plastic bowl with water from the canteen. She splashed her face, brushed her teeth, and tried to untangle her hair with a broken comb.

"Want some?" Poppy asked, holding out a crushed box of instant dry milk.

Ivy shook her head. She didn't want dry milk or old bread or another night in the cold. She wanted a house, and she wanted a dog.

Nearby, Poppy went through the same motions of shaking, smoothing, rolling his sleeping bag, splashing his face, brushing his teeth, and encountering the same frustration as Ivy.

The next order of business was to reach the shelter for breakfast. After that, Poppy planned to leave Ivy with one of the homeless mothers while he traipsed over to the unemployment office to check on jobs. He might also walk the streets, looking for HELP WANTED signs. Today he had a good feeling. Today he thought he would probably find work.

Since they had been homeless, getting to school had become extremely difficult. On days when Ivy did go to school, they had to rise in the dark to get to a shelter before the breakfast hour.

Because most shelters shut down for the day, the bathroom was always jammed in the early morning. People took turns bathing in the sink. There were no showers or tubs, and everyone was expected to bring a towel, for the shelters only provided paper napkins.

The women were often trying to get ready for work or job interviews. They had to fix their hair, put on make-up, polish their shoes, and press their clothes by stretching the wrinkles in all directions. They had to go to jobs, pretending they weren't homeless.

Ivy was no different. On school days she had to wait her turn at the sink, and the lines were always long. She had to brush out her hair, doff clean clothes, and go to school, pretending she wasn't homeless.

Ivy never mentioned to her teachers or friends what had happened to her — why they couldn't come over to play, why their phone didn't work, why she was often absent.

So far Ivy's most difficult moment at school proved to be the day the class had a project on HABITAT. They were asked to match a group of animals to the places they lived — lairs, caves, burrows, nests, warrens, and dens. They were also asked to check whether their family lived in a house, apartment, flat, loft, boat, or car.

"Who would live in a car?" One of Ivy's friends asked.

Ivy blushed with shame, for a lair and cave might best describe the places she had been sleeping lately. Certainly, apartment or loft did not fit at all.

Although Ivy and her father were homeless, she knew that her grandfather Bly had a large house in New York. All her relatives had grown up in houses — stone, wood, and brick houses. Poppy said her grandfather's house was a mansion and that he had more than one home. Supposedly, there were several Bly residences — one in Utah where he skied, one on an island near Florida, one in Texas where he raised horses, and one in New York with a tennis court and pool.

Ivy was never sure whether Poppy fabricated these stories, like the ones about their old red van. However, in the cold and dark, she pretended they were true. She dreamed of waking up in one of those beautiful, faraway dwellings. If her grandfather Bly had several homes with luxurious furnishings and elegant grounds, then surely she could claim one of them for her habitat. At school that day, Ivy lied and checked HOUSE.

Chapter 3

IVY AND POPPY PICKED THEIR WAY ACROSS THE WOODED EUCALYPTUS grove, heading towards the large boulevard that circled the west end of the city. Ivy carried two sleeping bags and tarps on a backpack frame bent to fit around her shoulders. Poppy carried the gear. Utensils, canned food, a box of dry milk, flashlight, candles, and matches were stuffed into a pack with pots and frying pans hanging off its side. He also held a metal box filled with tools, and each of them toted a small suitcase stuffed with personal belongings.

In Ivy's suitcase were her treasures. Prized above all were three obsidian rocks from Mount Shasta. Nine years ago, she had found them on the day she and Poppy scattered her mother's ashes on the side of that mountain. Next in importance was the red Swiss Army knife with three different blades and a tiny well for a plastic tooth-pick that Poppy had given her on her tenth birthday. There was also a box of paints, a wallet containing an outdated library card, a pad of drawing paper, and a calligraphy pen. Aside from a few articles of clothing, that was all.

Ivy turned around to utter one last good-bye to the dog who had been such a promising new friend, but he was no longer in sight. She inspected the hill, the gully, the base of the trees, but no dog. He had gone, disappeared, vanished. Disappointed, Ivy trudged up the embankment towards the city.

"I bet that dog brought us good luck, Poppy," Ivy said wishing to catch one more glimpse of that wiggling, wagging tail.

"Luck?" Poppy spit the word into the dirt. "I don't know what luck means anymore, princess."

"I do," she insisted. "I bet that dog was a lucky charm like a rabbit's foot or a four-leaf clover, and I bet you find a job today." Ivy whirled again in all directions. "But where has he run off to?"

As Ivy twirled back to the spot where she first spied the dog, she suddenly lost her footing. The backpack frame slipped off her shoulders as she tripped over her suitcase, scratched her face on the twigs that littered the hill, and hit her head on the edge of a large, protruding rock. Her suitcase opened, scattering its contents in all directions. Sleeping bags and tarps tumbled to the wayside, and she rolled to the bottom of a shallow ravine.

"Ivy princess! Ivy dear!" Poppy cried.

He threw down his suitcase and gear and plunged headlong down the hill. Two steep embankments formed the sides of the ravine, and at its bottom was an accumulation of dead leaves and mud.

"Ivy," Poppy murmured, but she did not respond. He lifted her eyelids, but her blank eyes saw nothing. She was unconscious.

From the gash on top of her head, blood streaked her hair. Poppy took a bandanna from his pocket and mopped the sticky liquid from Ivy's face. Then gently pulling the hair away, he bent in to get a closer look. The wound was bleeding profusely. However, on closer inspection, the cut didn't appear terribly serious.

More alarming than the blood and open skin was Ivy's unconscious condition. Her breathing was unsteady and erratic, her face ashen, her hands clammy, her legs loose. Poppy blew into her mouth and up her nostrils, trying to revive her.

"Help!" He muttered to the trees. Their soughing voices muttered back to him. "Surely," he said aloud, "someone can help us."

"Woof" was the welcome reply.

Their canine friend reappeared, and after surveying the heap of sleeping bags, the clothes flung far and wide, and Poppy's troubled, helpless look, he leapt through the rotten leaves and arrived at Ivy's side. Like a very efficient nurse, he immediately set about licking her head, cheeks, fingers, and ears.

"Good dog, good puppy dog. You can help Ivy, can't you? You can help bring her back?"

As the dog licked, Ivy's eyelids fluttered, but her body remained quiet and still.

Poppy began to cry, and the dog whimpered along in sympathy. Alternately, he lapped Poppy's salty tears and swabbed Ivy's lifeless face with his pink tongue.

Although it was barely past dawn, two men on off-trail mountain bicycles sped over the rough terrain towards Poppy, Ivy, and the dog. Covered in purple nylon tights, windbreakers, leather gloves, and bright yellow protection helmets, they screeched to a halt at the top of the hill to stare down at the miserable trio.

"What happened there?" They called.

"My daughter, my daughter," Poppy panicked.

One of the men jumped off his bike and tumbled down to Ivy's side. "Accident?" He asked, picking up her wrist and feeling her pulse. "Must have fallen, hey?"

"My little girl slipped and fell down the hill."

"Has she gone unconscious?" The other biker shouted down.

"That's right," Poppy confirmed, "and her head is cut."

"I don't think the wound is very deep," the biker said, inspecting Ivy's head. "But I'm afraid she may have a concussion."

Poppy looked at the two men helplessly.

"We'll ride to the nearest phone and call for help."

"Just had a bad fall, mister. She'll be all right."

The men adjusted their helmets and tightened the wristbands

of their gloves. "Try to keep her warm," they shouted as they took off through the eucalyptus grove.

Poppy removed Ivy's head from his lap and laid it on the ground. While he went to collect blankets from the bedroll and sleeping bags from the hillside, the dog snuggled firmly against the girl's chest. Again he licked the parts of Ivy's body he could reach, and when Poppy returned with the bedding, he licked him too.

"If you open your eyes, princess," Poppy whispered in a halting, broken voice, "you can see the hills of Angel Island. There's a large ship chugging towards the Port of Oakland, flying a light blue flag. It has come around the horn of Africa and through the Panama Canal. Open your eyes, Ivy," he coaxed softly, "and see the silver trusses of the Bay Bridge and the red cables of the Golden Gate."

The girl lay still.

"Princess Ivy, look up," Poppy pleaded, "and you'll see a little black and white dog. I promise he's right here."

With that the dog woofed once, and Ivy opened her eyes.

"Poppy," she cried, while father and dog smothered her with kisses and licks. "I was faraway, in a space ship, a ship that was moving slowly, as if it were traveling through mud. But we were really going thousands of miles an hour, and I could see the outline of the earth from my tiny window. The sun was an orange fire ball in the sky. It got bigger and closer, but I was freezing the whole time, trying to find a coat or blanket. I wanted to call your name, but I couldn't say it anymore. Then we were on Mount Shasta and mother was there. She was licking me, and every time her tongue touched my face, I got warm." Ivy paused to take a breath. "What happened?"

Poppy said, "Hush, baby! Hush, hush! It's all better now."

"But then, I started to float back down to earth. It was horrible at first, but mother came and everything was better. Did I fall?"

"You slipped, dear. You tumbled down the hill and cut your head. It knocked you out." Poppy exhaled a loud sigh of relief. "I was scared sick when you went unconscious."

"I was searching for you," Ivy eyed the little dog with reproval. "Yes, it's all your fault, for I was looking to tell you good-bye."

"He found you." Poppy leaned over Ivy's body and gave the dog a good rub. "He has been nursing you all along."

The dog slid a few inches forward, nuzzling Ivy's ribs. "You know he wants to be with us," she said half-heartedly. "You know that for sure."

The lines in Poppy's forehead deepened with a dozen objections. He pulled Ivy closer to him and whispered, "No way, princess. Not today."

Poppy said no more. He had already explained a situation which needed no explaining. The shelters didn't permit animals. Food was scarce enough. The prospects of finding a place to live in the near future were slim. What more could he say? Worst of all, what more could he do?

"Just because I understand why we can't have a dog doesn't mean I have to accept it."

Poppy fully agreed. There were many things about their situation which he understood, but that didn't make it easier.

"Sometimes all the understanding in the world doesn't help," he said resentfully. After all, he had tried to get a job and couldn't. He understood that. He had tried to raise his daughter decently and now that was failing too. Although more families were homeless and jobs hard to get, it didn't make him accept the conditions of it any easier. The bitterness of their predicament flooded his heart.

"Things are going to get better, princess," Poppy forced himself to say. "Then we can get a dog. Then we can buy you a parakeet and a horse too."

Ivy smiled weakly. Her father was better at making promises than keeping them, but it was the best he could do these days. Making promises for the future was the only fun they had.

"I love you, Princess Ivy."

Ivy rested in Poppy's arms, while the dog ran in circles, pleased that the young girl had finally woken up. Eventually, he tired and collapsed on Ivy's chest, motionless except for his perpetually wagging tail.

Only the distant sound of roaring sirens broke the serenity. The persistent noise grew louder and closer until the whirring sounds stopped nearby. Cars honked, brakes screeched, and through the trees Poppy could distinguish the red flashing lights of emergency vehicles.

"Must have been a bad accident up there," Poppy commented quietly. "We might as well wait here for a while. Let you rest and let them clear it up. No matter what, the shelter will be closed for breakfast by the time we get over there." Poppy reached into his pocket and jangled a few quarters in change. "How does a trip to the donut shop sound?"

That sounded like a promise Poppy could keep.

Above the ravine and through the thick grove of trees, policemen and ambulance drivers trod through the brush.

"Hello! Hello!" A policeman shouted through a megaphone, "Anybody hurt down there?"

The ambulance men followed closely behind. "Did somebody call 911?" They shouted. "Does somebody need an ambulance?"

The outlines of the figures moved slowly but surely in their direction, continuing to call, "Did somebody call 911?"

Ivy clung to Poppy's neck in terror. She was afraid of the police, social workers, and the authorities who might take her away from her father. Her biggest fear was being removed from Poppy's care. She knew that homeless kids were often taken away if their parents were unfit or vagrants.

In the dictionary, it said "vagrant" was an "idle wanderer" or a "tramp." Poppy wasn't idle or a tramp, but that didn't console Ivy. She knew that with his worn-out clothes and long hair, he looked like a vagrant. She knew that vagrancy was sometimes considered a crime, especially if you had a child.

Poppy's fears were identical. It was hard for single fathers to keep their children with them. The best-kept homeless shelters were reserved for women and children. A few months ago the police had stopped and asked Ivy if Poppy were really her father. The officer had wanted to run Poppy in for questioning about a Monterey County kidnaping that had happened six years ago. The police said Ivy resembled the girl who had disappeared. Poppy had waved Ivy's birth certificate at the officers until they let him go.

Now the ambulance crew was fully visible. Poppy held his fingers to his lips to quiet the restless pup. Ivy buried herself deep into her father's lap, hoping to hide, while Poppy frantically searched the hillside, looking for an escape.

Chapter 4

DESPITE IVY'S SHAKY CONDITION, THE ONLY THING TO DO WAS bolt. Poppy decided the best route was to scramble over several boulders and head down to the water.

"Let's get going," he pressed urgently. Poppy climbed over the first rock. "Follow me," he said, indicating a path that led directly to the bay.

Meanwhile in the opposite direction, the little dog trotted confidently into a tall eucalyptus thicket. The grey bark of the trees hung in loose skin off the trunks, and a strong medicinal aroma thickened the air. After the dog entered the grove, he turned back and cocked his head to one side, as if to ask, "What are you two waiting for? Aren't you coming with me?"

"That way," Ivy pointed to their four-legged friend, "he's telling us to go that way."

"I don't think that leads anywhere, except trouble." Poppy looked skeptically at the thick undergrowth covered with fresh winter patches of poison oak.

The dog's head angled further to his side, resting almost on his paws while the question in his eyes grew insistent.

"Come on, Poppy," Ivy said impatiently. "The pup is waiting for us." Ivy's instincts told her if they wanted to escape from the police and avoid inquiries about vagrancy, she and Poppy must follow the mysterious little dog. She tugged on her father's fingers, and while his arm leaned in her direction, nothing else budged. Ivy looked at her father with dismay. This was no time to stop and consider other possibilities. At that instant she dropped Poppy's hand and took off through the woods.

"Ivy," Poppy whispered in frustration, "come back."

The backsides of Ivy and the dog retreated into the brush and out of sight. Poppy now had no other choice but to follow.

The thick woods divided on either side of a narrow footpath which wove like the curve of a snake. The path was barely visible and dead, dried brambles were piled high along its edges. However, the shouts of the ambulance drivers and police, the sounds of sirens and horns were soon muffled in the distance.

Occasionally, the woods would open, and Ivy could glimpse the steely waters of the bay or the stern of a freighter, but they usually moved along, enveloped by thick forest growth. Over them the tops of the conifers formed a green canopy, and rays of sun winked warmly through the pine boughs.

More than once Poppy asked himself where they would end up, how they would get back to camp to collect their gear, if Ivy's head needed medical attention, where he was going to find a job, when they would get some breakfast, and most of all, why in the world they were following a dumb, mute, canine creature through the woods to an unknown destination?

"Ivy," Poppy called ahead, "let's go back to the camp now. Surely the police have left."

In answer, the dog barked out, as if to say, "Just a bit further, just a wee little bit."

"Ivy," Poppy said, "we need to get back and collect our sleeping bags now."

Frantic feelings had started to brew inside Poppy's head. They needed the bags and gear for their survival. It was too cold at night to go without covering, and during the winter season it was almost impossible to find room in a homeless shelter. They would be in serious trouble if the police had confiscated their belongings for identification.

Poppy turned in the direction of the camp just as the dog woofed loudly. He looked to see that the path had abruptly ended in the backyard of a pink stucco mansion. Drapes covered most of the glass, and heavy scrolls of wrought-iron bars crossed the windows. Rows of terra cotta tiles, some broken or missing, composed the roof. Two chimneys towered above the crumbling two-story structure. Wispy smoke curled from one, and from the top of the other, a weathercock swung in the crisp, chilly wind.

The dog nudged open a rotten wooden gate and briskly crossed the lawn to the steps of the back porch.

"You stay right here, young lady." Poppy gripped Ivy's elbow in his hand while he considered the dilemma before them. Vagrancy was one sort of crime, but trespassing on private property, especially rich people's property, was quite another. There appeared no way to scoot around to the street without passing closely to the house itself. That could mean serious danger if an alarm system, guards, a lunatic with a gun, or vicious dogs happened to be on the premises. Poppy wouldn't want to risk any of those.

"Crrsseechhh," the dog scratched away at the screen door, dragging its paw across the metal mesh. "Crseech, crseech." A rip in the screen fit exactly with the pup's rhythmic downstroke.

"Is that ye out there? Making a racket to raise the dead?"

From inside the house came the loud rattle of locks and chains, and a tall, erect old woman appeared in the frame of the door.

"I know ye can hear me coming from a mile away," an unnaturally strong voice boomed out of her withered body, "but ye has to go on scratching the day and door away, even if ye got the ears of a creature that hears me tying my shoes on the second floor. I ought to turn ye out for good, turn ye out to fend for yeself. Yes, that's what I ought to do. Raising the dead with ye ornery foot."

The woman was as old as anything Ivy had ever seen, but her voice was resonant like a girl's, thick with textures that made her words sound like waves or water. These words, as she said them, sang out in loud, lilting melodies.

"Ye coming back from those nightly haunts, are ye?"

The dog's tail wagged happily in response to the odd woman's comment, question, and criticism.

The wizened thing continued, her voice rising and falling like a fountain. "I know where ye been. Out in those woods there ye have, out there bothering every other thing that lives, instead of staying home where ye should be resting and bothering the likes of me."

Suddenly the tail, followed by the dog's entire body, fell back in exhaustion on the porch step.

"I worries about ye when ye disappear like that, my little friend Dice, my fellow creature, alone and alive in the big world. Off ye go without so much as a merry-ye-know. Ye knows I worry, don't ye?"

The dog's tail thumped and wagged.

"Dice, Dice, Dice!" The woman trilled.

Ivy ogled the dog's black spots. The big dark ones contrasted with the white ones and within each one of the larger spots, there were little specks of contrasting colors. "Dice," the girl sighed with pleasure.

The dog's head turned pridefully towards Ivy, as if to say, "Yes, that is my beautiful name, and you can stop calling me 'dog' now."

"If ye aren't one of the wonders, Dice? Now what did ye bring me this time?" The old woman asked.

Dice cocked his head.

"Ye aren't going deaf on me, are ye?" Her voice boomed louder than ever. "I said, what did ye bring me from ye outing in the woods?"

Dice's tail clacked on the stairs as loudly as the old woman's voice.

"Did ye bring me an acorn? Or a giant mushroom? Did ye bring me the stem of a wild iris? Tell me, Dice, my little friend, my fellow creature. Ye know I'm too old to go roaming myself. My roaming and wandering days are almost over."

As Dice's head turned, the woman's large watery grey eyes followed. There before her were the figures of Poppy and Ivy on the other side of her rickety gate.

"See," Dice's tail wagged, as if to say, "I've brought you them."

The old woman lifted a pair of spectacles suspended around her neck and peered with great surprise. She smoothed down her black crepe dress, patted a few stray hairs into the bun at the nape of her neck, and twisted her head to ascertain that what stood before her was real.

"Real fellow human creatures?" The woman's eyes steadied first on Poppy and then on Ivy, flitting back and forth from face to face. "Oh, Dice, we've been so lonely here."

Dice nodded in full agreement.

"Ye speak, don't ye?" The old woman bellowed across the yard. "Ye speak English?"

Poppy nodded, still speechless.

"Yes, of course, we speak English," Ivy said defiantly. "Poppy speaks French too."

"Well, 'bon jour' to ye too."

Poppy stood rigid and silent.

"Don't stand there like ye was deaf and dumb! Come over here!" The woman's invitation was rough and rude, and her index finger wriggled up and down like a queen's scepter. "What are ye standing way over by the gate for? Ye talk, don't ye?"

Poppy hesitated, insulted by the tone. After all, they were not vagrants, strays, or bums. He expected to be treated with a little respect.

"Tiger got ye tongue?"

Ivy made a motion to enter through the gate, but Poppy forced her back.

"What are ye afraid of, sir?" The old woman's voice had not

diminished its volume, but the tone had softened into politeness.

"Not afraid," Poppy said calmly. "We followed your dog here, but now I think we'll trot back to where we came from?"

The old woman laughed like an ignited cannonball. "Trotting after that Dice, no doubt. If he's the one ye follow, it will take the wind out of ye sails."

"I mean we'll 'go' back to where we came from," Poppy corrected, while his face flamed with embarrassment.

"And where might that be? Ireland with that wild strawberry hair? Or Russia, sir? Ye might originate in Italy? The Renaissance or the Bel Epoch? Tell me where ye people came from and tell me what year they came. Then I shall tell ye that there is none of us who can go back. Not even me, who was born in Scotland and lived there when I was a wee little girl. We are Americans now. Isn't that right, Dice?"

The dog's tail thumped once.

"Dice knows when I am correct. At my age no telling what I get wrong — grocery lists, days of the week, starch in the shirts, friends' birthdays and deathdays. But with the most important items, I still got my faculties straight. Sound right, sir?"

Poppy did not answer.

"Afraid to talk to me yet, are ye?"

"Not afraid. Just thinking the girl and I ought to be heading back through the woods."

"Ye are welcome to come in, if ye like. We like a visit, we do."

Poppy was a shy man, and the company of strangers did not suit him. He had met too many of them these last few months, looking for work and shelter. However, it might be best to go inside, wash off Ivy's cut, and plan how best to retrieve their things.

While Ivy waited for Poppy to decide what to do, she counted the windows in the two stories of the imposing old house — ten large ones in the back plus six French doors. In addition, a round dormer in the apex of the roof promised a big, drafty attic. Heavy floral curtains and sand-colored Venetian blinds over the windows and doors blocked any view into the house.

The exterior was in grave disrepair. The visible glass was caked with dirt and dust. The paint was stripped from the door and window moldings. All the screens were ripped. The black wrought-iron was weathered down to flat grey. The stucco was puckered and discolored. The lawn and garden were untended, and although there were a few stray winter blooms on the rose bushes, their stems straggled at awkward angles, begging to be pruned.

"Suit yeself, but ye are most welcome to come into the house." The old woman opened the backdoor for Dice to enter. "Suit yeself," she repeated, "but there's donuts and hot cocoa before ye go on ye way."

Chapter 5

MISS EUGENIA ORR LEANED ON A CARVED EBONY CANE AND led Ivy and Poppy onto her small screen porch.

"Ivy Bly," Miss Orr pronounced the three syllables with care, "and Mister Poppy Bly, welcome."

"They're coming in," Dice yelped, running around in circles and barking ecstatically. "They're coming into my house."

On the porch, Ivy and Poppy had to wind through aisles of cartons, stacks of canned foods, and cases of bottled water. Aside from the food supplies, a pink wicker chaise-lounge covered in tattered, mildew pillows took up the far corner, and by it were the frames of two rusty bicycles.

"Is this a shelter?" Ivy inquired, squeezing past the towering boxes of food.

"Shelter, child?" Miss Orr pondered the question. "Shelter, ummmm? Let me see what ye might mean."

Miss Orr appeared to examine the word "shelter" as if it clung to the air, while Ivy examined Miss Orr. The old creature's grey eyes looked dazed and distant behind her glasses, but as soon as she focused their attention, the grey deepened into violet. Her glasses conveniently rested on one delicate hump while her nose sloped gracefully towards her enormous mouth. Perhaps the dimensions of the mouth had something to do with the volume of the voice, for her lips revealed an elasticity that stretched in all directions. As for her skin, it was wrinkled with age, but its creases, moles, and imperfections were covered with thick powder topped by dabs of rouge. Her ears drooped with heavy gold filigree earrings. As for her hair, it was hard for Ivy to look at all. Pulled back into a bun and tightly clasped with a large gold barrette, it appeared to be smeared haphazardly with black shoe polish. The roots looked tortured, and as she spoke, Miss Orr nervously felt for any hairs that might have gone astray.

Her hands! On every crinkled finger was a gold ring with a dazzling stone. The emerald was deep and quiet. The ruby throbbed with redness. The sapphire was the color of her grey-blue-violet eyes. The diamond was as clear as water. The pearl rose like a bubble of champagne.

However, Miss Orr's rings were the only gaudy thing about her. She wore an old, black crepe dress with a round white collar, and a yellow sweater, as pale as the color of the sun covered with clouds. The dress descended to her ankles which were protected by thick white cotton socks, and on her feet was a pair of worn red Chinese slippers.

"Shelter from the cold?" Miss Orr's voice reverberated more loudly indoors, and Dice covered his ears with his paws. "Shelter from the storms and shelter from the night? Is that what ye mean by shelter, child?"

"Not exactly," Ivy said, scanning the boxes of canned peas, creamed corn, condensed milk, ketchup, olives, kippers, and apple sauce.

"Oh, ye must be talking about the supplies, child. Those are what we call 'emergency rations,' and ye don't live as long as I have without running out of food. I have survived two Great Wars on sight and several minor skirmishes. For the last sixty-six years, I've kept adequate supplies on hand at all times. When I traveled around the world, I carried an entire trunk of canned goods and always had the most quarrelsome times at customs. They are so fussy, those customs men. Does that answer ye question?"

Miss Orr peered at Ivy's bright green eyes, roamed the circumference of her soiled, tired face, and looked at her wild, gnarled, tangled, bloody hair. Then she lighted on Ivy's ruby-colored birthmark. "Look here, child, an angel kissed me too."

Ivy's mouth widened in amazement. No one but Poppy had ever called her birthmark "the kiss of an angel."

Miss Orr shoved her tiny, wizened cheek at Ivy, and her gold earrings jangled in the girl's ear. Underneath the layer of soft powder was a pink star, much like Ivy's own.

"Here ye go. Ye can touch it with ye finger, if ye please."

"No, thank you," Ivy faltered.

"Don't thank me, thank yeself. Ye was one who was kissed by angels. I know nothing better for coming into the world."

Ivy nodded at the old woman with embarrassment. Frankly, she could have imagined a few things better than a discolored mark on her face.

"Ye mark will take good care of ye the way mine has taken care of me. Not to fret, child."

Miss Orr pointed to a box of marshmallows with her cane. "These we put next to the chocolate syrup," she said. "I have such a weakness for my sweets, and so does Dice. He is very fond of gummy bears, the green ones in particular, which roll between his teeth like marbles."

While Miss Orr chattered, Poppy watched the sky through the screen door. The morning blue was now streaked with grey clouds and a v-shaped flock of tardy geese hurried their way south. Poppy's better judgment was to leave this strange old woman to her dog and move across the wild yard, through the gate, and onto the footpath that led back through the woods. Still, he did not stir.

"Ye are welcome to leave anytime the notion takes ye," Miss Orr said, as if reading Poppy's mind. "But for now, let us do as I promised. That is, if ye want a cup of something hot to drink and a donut to fill ye breakfast belly."

Dice joggled his tail at the mention of food and rushed ahead of the old woman, barking, "I am the hungriest beast here."

"Now, Dice," Miss Orr thumped her cane, "ye almost knocked me into the beans."

Ivy looked at the lettering scrawled across the cartons by the kitchen door. PINTO, NAVY, KIDNEY, LIMA, and LENTILS were written in large block letters.

"Ye can have a can of those little white beans, the ones they call navy, with ye donut if ye want. They're not as bad a combination as ye may think. I can tell ye that truthfully, for I've been eating beans and donuts for close to fifty-seven years. Yes, next week marks the day in London when I had my first such meal. The bombs were falling left, the bombs were falling right, and I survived the day which I am most sad to report was not the fate of many others. I have been devoted to the duo ever since."

Ivy smiled politely and looked to Poppy for a cue. He slyly patted his stomach in anticipation of breakfast.

In the kitchen the overhead light reflected across the dingy lime green walls. White curtains, soiled to putty grey, framed the windows, and behind the dirty glass hung the wrought-iron bars. A chipped wooden table sat forlornly in the center surrounded by several misassorted chairs. The green linoleum tiles on the floor were cracked. The stove was encrusted with old food. The sink was piled high with dishes. The exterior of the refrigerator was streaked with the debris of long-ago eaten repasts. Several cupboards had lost their doors. Grease stains on the clock made it difficult to tell the time, and the wall calendar nearby said FEBRUARY 1952.

Instead of smelling of warm things to eat, the kitchen stank of dust and sour milk.

Ivy was severely disappointed. From the grand scale of the house, the size of the grounds, the evidence of the homes nearby, she thought that she was entering a rich woman's domain. Instead, it was a huge mess.

Poppy, on the other hand, was rather cheered. It was the first time he had been inside a building in two days.

"How long have you lived here?" Poppy asked Miss Orr.

The old woman's eyes flew to the calendar on the wall. Over boxes marked with days of the week was the faded outline of a standard black poodle standing in front of the Eiffel Tower.

"February," she said decisively. "It was February 1952." And pointing to the calendar, added, "I left it up the first day that we moved in here so I wouldn't forget. Do ye think that was clever?"

"Nineteen fifty-two was before Poppy was born," Ivy said.

"Many things happened before ye Poppy was born, child." Miss Orr smiled with her large mouth, and her lips stretched to her ears, showing off a set of perfect pearl-white teeth. Like her voice, the woman's teeth were seventy years younger than the rest of her. "But the event of ye Poppy's birth — that was unique. It only happened once, and it will never happen again."

"Yes," Ivy reflected, "that's true."

"Wouldn't ye know?" Miss Orr continued, "It's February again. We've had us a mild winter, but a storm is about to blow in. I feel it in my knees here. They get creaky before a big one."

Poppy looked anxiously through the dirty kitchen windows. Grey speckled the blue sky, and gusty winds had started to toy with the large trees in the yard.

Miss Orr took a battered copper kettle and filled it with water. From the cupboard she lifted out a dented tin that pictured a dancing Aztec princess and the letters C O C O A. From inside the refrigerator, she pulled out a box large enough to hold several dozen donuts.

"Now that I have told how long I have lived in this house, ye tell me, Ivy, how many years, months, weeks ago ye were born?"

Wavering for a moment, Ivy calculated, "Twelve years, five months, two weeks, and three days." Then, turning to Poppy, "What time of day was I born, Poppy?"

"On the stroke of noon," he smiled.

"Three days, ten hours, and three minutes."

"Good," cheered Miss Orr. "I can see ye was born with sense in your head. Ye have already lived a million seconds, for that is a mere ten days. As for a billion, that takes around thirty years. But can ye guess how long are a trillion seconds?"

Ivy was stumped.

"Twenty-eight thousand years!" Miss Orr's head bobbed. "Too long for one lifetime."

"I also know the names of birds and flowers," Ivy boasted, "and the words to two songs in French."

Ivy spotted Poppy's reproachful look. He hated when she bragged.

"Let her boast a little, Mister Poppy," Miss Orr declared with authority. "I can see that she is proud of what ye taught her."

Poppy's irritation with the old woman's manner was checked by the smell of warm cocoa. Putting up with Miss Orr was a small price to pay for breakfast which as soon as they had eaten, Poppy told himself, they would leave.

Judging from the sky, the sooner the better. It now threatened to rain. Poppy grew as gloomy as the day. Everything they owned was lying on a hillside, if the police hadn't picked through it. If they were lucky, their items were still there, but if the sky continued to darken, their bedding would soon be soaked and their few clothes ruined.

"Can you lift this, child?" Miss Orr handed the girl a red lacquered tray. Three white porcelain bowls were filled with steamy fresh cocoa, and on top of each chocolate pond a marshmallow drifted back and forth like a water lily.

"We'll be taking our cocoa French-style, if ye don't mind," Miss Orr said agreeably, meaning that in France adults and children mixed coffee and milk together in bowls in which they dipped their morning bread.

Poppy sighed aloud. It was no wonder Miss Orr did not mind Ivy boasting. Miss Eugenia Orr was capable of doing a bit of boasting herself.

A dozen custard-filled donuts were arranged in stacks on a tarnished silver platter, as well as a pitcher of orange juice, a box of cereal, a bottle of cream, and two demi-tasse cups of espresso coffee.

"We have not had visitors here at *Tosca* in an age. How thrilling to think that we now have two."

"*Tosca?*" The word bubbled over lemon cream, dough, and powdered sugar.

"Don't talk with your mouth full," Poppy snapped. He was sipping the first espresso coffee he had had in three months, and if it hadn't been for the impending storm, he would have thoroughly enjoyed it.

"What's *Tosca?*" Ivy asked.

"*Tosca* is the name of an opera," Poppy rejoined, wanting Miss Orr to know that she wasn't the only one at the table with manners and education.

"Bravo! Bravo, Mister Poppy!" Miss Orr's hands clapped quickly and lightly, and the sound fluttered through the room like a flock of birds. "The name of an opera," she continued, "and the name of this house. When we first came here, in what year did I say?" She glanced at the calendar. "Yes, in 1952, it was called *The Palms*, but we immediately changed it to *Tosca*. Ye see, child, *Tosca* was my favorite role," she uttered wistfully.

A song burst from Miss Orr's thin chest, and she heaved out a string of words in a foreign language that Ivy did not understand.

The beautiful song made Ivy long to ask Miss Orr what the words signified, what "we" referred to when she mentioned moving to *Tosca*, and what her "favorite role" could possibly mean.

Ivy kept these questions to herself and instead hurried to finish breakfast. From the worried look in Poppy's eye, she could see that as soon as they had made a proper thank-you and good-bye, they would be back out in the cold.

Chapter 6

"I'M NO LONGER IN THE MOOD FOR TALKING," MISS ORR announced in her high, girlish voice, pouring more coffee and cocoa into their cups. "I've talked off both ye ears," and with that, she tossed her hands into the air, letting the glitter of her rings catch the overhead light.

Once more a short song flew out of Miss Orr's throat. It was a pure, beautiful sound in a voice that didn't sound real. In fact, nothing seemed real. Ivy felt the table to see if it was wood. Yes, real wood, she affirmed. She touched her arm which responded as skin. She reached up to her head and felt the matted blood from her fall earlier that morning. Dice was real. She could reach under the table with her foot and feel his silly wagging tail.

Then Ivy looked at Miss Orr's hair. It wasn't real. It was shoe polish. She watched Miss Orr's mouth open and close around the high notes of her song, which didn't look real either. She inspected the kitchen. It was a soiled storybook picture.

As Miss Orr sang, Ivy rubbed her eyes. Nothing went away. She closed them again, placed her head across her folded arms, and let the *bel canto* song waft around her.

Suddenly, the voice reached above high C and a wine glass shattered on the floor.

"My! Oh my! Oh my! Oh my! Crystal stemware given to me by the daughter of the Duchess of Orleans. That's the last of it, alas the last. The last! The last!"

"Ooohh!" Ivy murmured sympathetically, "I'm sorry."

"But there's nothing ye can do. It's broken and gone, like so many other things." Miss Orr dabbed at her tear-filled eyes.

Dice scampered out of the kitchen while Poppy found a weathered broom. Its straws had all been broken or bent, and its slim, wooden handle was nicked and chipped.

"It was a beautiful song, Miss Orr," Poppy said, sweeping the shards of tinkling crystal into a pile. Ivy thought there was more glass in the pieces than in the whole.

"Thank ye, Mister Poppy, thank ye but ye are too kind." Miss Orr smiled graciously, "I'm afraid most of the voice is gone like the stemware."

"Is that really your last?" Ivy asked.

"My last voice, child? Or my last song?"

"Your last piece of crystal given to you by the daughter of the Duchess of Orleans?"

"Yes, that's all of the set," the old woman nodded fitfully. "Originally, there were twelve, but I have broken them, one by one, whenever I've gone after that E flat. However, I am not crying, child. On the contrary. I am laughing, for it all goes in time — the crystal and the high notes."

"Amen," Poppy muttered, calculating his own losses in the

world, hoping he might soon count his bad luck behind him.

Miss Orr tapped her heart, "Everything but the music goes, for that is stored in here." Then her voice lifted forcefully again, "When one thing goes, something else arrives, child. Never doubt that. Something mysterious and unexpected is surely coming for all of us."

"Like a good kick in the pants," Poppy said gruffly.

"I hope not, Mister Poppy, but look what a splendid job ye have done with the breakage. I don't know how to thank ye for helping clean things up. I am too old to get things properly done."

At first Poppy simply flushed with embarrassment and said nothing, but soon his lips began to shape words through his beard. Ivy heard his intelligent, measured voice, and she thought that her father was an elegant man, despite his rags and empty pockets.

"Please don't mention it, Miss Orr," he stuttered, "for we are strangers, and you have kindly asked us into your home."

"I did not think a thing of it, Mister Poppy. Dice invited ye here, and I trust he wouldn't bring evil to my doorstep."

Dice trotted in from the hall to accept the words of praise. However, much to Ivy's regret, Poppy now rose to go. "Miss Orr, thank you, but we must be going."

Ivy scowled. After all, what awaited her outside was a cold, winter day, turning windy and probably turning wet. At best, Ivy might pass the afternoon at the community center on Mission Street, taking care of a couple of brats. At worst, she would spend it with Poppy roaming around town, looking for work. She had run out of good books to read, her library card had expired, and it was impossible to renew one without a home address. Now her paints and prized possessions were all lost in the woods, and she had nothing with which to amuse herself.

"What is ye line of work, Mister Poppy?" Miss Orr inquired, accompanying father and daughter to the back door.

"He's excellent at cleaning up, Miss Orr," Ivy bragged. "He can do anything, fix anything, make anything. He's very handy."

"Ivy," Poppy said, "we are leaving now. Say good-bye to Miss Orr."

Ivy froze.

"Get your jacket on," Poppy instructed. "We must hurry along."

Miss Orr's head lifted quizzically at an angle, like a bird listening for its mate or like Dice in the woods. Ivy cocked her head too to register the distant but steady sound approaching from deep inside the house. Slow, heavy, cumbersome steps could be heard descending an uncarpeted staircase, steps which came closer and closer until a gigantic man, tall as well as broad and almost as ancient as Miss Orr herself, filled the entire doorway to the kitchen.

Not a shred of hair showed on his head, and the top of it glowed like a lightbulb. However, he sported a long moustache that curled at the ends, thick glasses, a silk printed robe, and red Chinese slippers three times as big as Miss Orr's. A fat, unlit cigar hung between his soft lower lip and snowy moustache.

"I'd like ye to meet my baby brother," Miss Orr said. "Mister Oscar Orr, meet Mister Poppy and his daughter, Ivy, and welcome them to *Tosca.*"

Oscar Orr bowed at the waist, and a protruding network of blue veins bulged through the top of his bald head.

"Mister Poppy Bly and daughter Ivy, meet my baby brother, Mister Oscar Orr," Miss Orr repeated.

"Sister, lower your voice," Oscar pleaded in a whisper, for his voice was as small as his body was big.

"How do ye do?" He said softly, turning to Ivy and Poppy. "How do ye do? How do ye do? Welcome to *Tosca.* By the way, my big sister Eugenia cannot hear a blasted thing. She has only two blasted channels. Either she is shouting or she is singing."

"I can hear as well as I blasted please," Miss Orr yelled in response.

"But when exactly is it ye pleases?" Oscar Orr pointed his cigar in indignation. "Yes, Eugenia, doing what she pleases. Well, do ye think it pleases our guests to have ye shouting and thundering all over the neighborhood like a fisherman's wife?"

On cue Miss Orr broke into the line of a ditty,

> *Singing cockles and mussels*
> *Alive, alive — Oooooooohhhhhh!*

The *Oooooooohhhhhh!* went on for a full minute, and several cats in the next room let out a howl.

Oscar threw up his hands, stuck his cigar into the pocket of his silk robe, and shuffled over to the pot of espresso coffee. After pouring its remains into a bowl, he added quantities of sugar and milk, dumped in three glazed donuts, and mashed the concoction together like mush. He then sat down the portion of himself that could fit onto a wooden chair, lifted his snowy mustache with one hand, and spooned mouthfuls from the bowl into his mouth.

"When ye shall stop smoking those foul cigars," Miss Orr pouted, "then I shall stop shouting. That Turkish tobacco irritates my epiglottis in the winter when we can't keep the windows open."

"Sister, ye have been complaining about ye epiglottis since ye were born, but it probably fell out a quarter of a century ago." Oscar muttered between bites. "You know, I am patient, but your shouting tries my patience. After all, I am a mortal man, not a saint."

"We are well aware of that, my dear brother." Miss Orr stuck her tongue out at Oscar, and Oscar flicked his nose with his thumb in a rude reply.

"I have tolerated ye cigars beyond a half century. Ye can at least understand that when I speak, when I sing, I want to be sure the world can hear me."

"Sister, we hear ye." Turning to Ivy and Poppy, he whispered, "We hear her, don't we?"

Ivy and Poppy agreed.

Miss Orr lowered her voice to a normal pitch. "Like this?"

They nodded again.

"Like this?" She whispered.

Everyone nodded.

"I never believe my baby brother. During our years together on the stage, Oscar teased me unmercifully. I finally refused to listen to anything he said. But today, I shall listen to ye." Miss Orr bowed.

As Poppy again made a move to go, Dice trooped back to his spot underneath the kitchen table, and Oscar started another pot of coffee.

"Dice brought them to *Tosca*," Miss Orr announced.

"Brought whom?" Oscar asked.

"The man over there and his daughter."

"Brought them from where?" Oscar fixed on Poppy's ragged clothes.

"I haven't asked," Miss Orr said, shocked at her oversight. "Where did Dice find ye?"

"On the west end of the park," Poppy said. "Now we had better hurry back to collect our things before a storm blows in."

"But where do they usually stay?" Oscar asked.

"I did not inquire that either," Miss Orr apologized.

"Don't ye think it rude not to ask the basics?"

"Yes, of course, but we have been having such a good time, I forgot." She added, "I did ask what sort of donut they preferred."

"Sister, ye were always a peculiar hostess. Next time they come, ye must ask them where they live."

"We really will be going now," Poppy said again, "and we do thank you for your hospitality."

"Thank you," Ivy chirped.

"Wherever it is ye are going," Miss Orr shouted Poppy down as he stepped out the door, "my brother Oscar is glad to drive ye. Wherever it is ye live, he would be delighted to take ye over there. Wouldn't you, brother?"

Oscar's mouth was full, and by the time he had chewed and swallowed his food, Poppy had mounted a protest. "No, that is much too much trouble. We couldn't possibly accept."

"Of course, ye can," Miss Orr retorted. "Since we let our chauffeur go, ye see, Oscar does all the driving. He is an excellent steering and brake man. In fact, I tell him if the boy hadn't played the violin so well, he might have been a racing driver. When we watch the Grand Prix, I remind Oscar what a marvelous driver he is. Ye would be perfectly safe in a car under his hand."

Poppy stammered out a reply. "We can manage ourselves."

"We know that, but ye have fallen on hard times, haven't ye?" Miss Orr boomed.

"We are getting by," Poppy said proudly, patting Ivy's head. "This one's a good girl, and I can count on her."

"Ye look like hard times themselves," Oscar volunteered his opinion. "Bad luck or good luck, ye never know. Some good might come from it after all. Don't let sister frighten ye to death. I would be glad to give ye a ride to ye house or ye things or wherever ye need be going. I have got to go out so it's nothing at all."

Once more Poppy surveyed the sky. The morning blue had altogether vanished and been replaced with the tarnished grey of polished pewter. Clouds accumulated in large puffs directly above them. A few raindrops splashed the dirty windows and streaked their dust. Then the entire canopy of heaven opened like a geyser. The overhead lights flickered, and thunder rolled through the halls. Dice growled, and the cats joined him in their yowling. Poppy, Ivy, Miss Orr, and her brother Oscar stood at the back door watching the rain slap the grass in the yard. The rose bushes bent to the ground, and the pale pink petals from the few remaining blossoms were torn away. Trickling gullies of water formed along the broken walkways and rushed towards them.

"The winter rains," Poppy mumbled in despair. The winter rains had returned, and where would he and Ivy go now?

Chapter 7

I T WAS JUST AS MISS ORR CLAIMED. HER BROTHER OSCAR swerved the wheels and floored the accelerator like a race-car driver. In his powder-blue 1954 Cadillac, an automobile as big as a small dwelling, Mr. Orr tore out of the garage into the beating rain, careened down the driveway onto the street, screamed around several corners into a large boulevard, and headed west to the out-skirts of San Francisco.

The Cadillac's interior was immaculate, sparkling with care. The midnight blue upholstery was in pristine condition, its fabric made of soft, luxuriant material. The dials were polished, the dash-board dusted and encased in dark blue leather, the fixtures encir-cled with shining chrome, and mounted on the glove compartment was a plaque engraved in script —

This El Dorado Cadillac belongs to Eugenia Orr

In contrast, the car's exterior was full of holes and dents. Each of the fenders was crumpled, and all four doors were mashed. The windshield had tiny spiderweb cracks on the passenger side, and all that remained of the sideview mirror was a chrome frame and a menacing sliver of glass.

From her place in the back, Ivy draped her arms around Poppy's neck, clutching her father like a drowning cat, while Poppy held onto the overhead strap with a feeling of desperation.

Oscar leaned his big body forward onto the steering wheel so he could see out the window. He rubbed the inside of the foggy windshield with his greasy palm, which removed traces of donuts but in no way improved visibility. It was likely he was almost blind in clear, sunny weather, and the inclemency of this day would strain anyone's eyes. Twice his large belly depressed the horn and caused Ivy to rise violently, banging her head against the padded ceiling of the car.

"Perhaps you had better slow down," Poppy urged.

"What did ye say?" Oscar asked, for there was no way he could hear anything above the noise of the storm and the car stopping, squeaking, starting, and sputtering.

"SLOW DOWN," Poppy yelled.

"I believe the speedometer is broken," Oscar admitted. "It says we are traveling zero miles per hour, which could not possibly be correct."

"Mr. Orr," Poppy loosened Ivy's strangulating arms and gasped for breath, "would you mind if I drove?" Poppy was emphatic. "I am a very careful driver."

At that moment, the right front tire ran over the curb. "That was a close one," Oscar admitted, pulling the car onto the straightaway. "Bad luck, good luck? Ye never know. Lucky for us no one was parked there."

The rain beat as heavy as bricks on the roof of the car, and trickles of water streaked horizontally across its windows.

"I can see in this weather," Poppy continued confidently. "I have excellent eyes so how about pulling over in this filling station and letting me drive?" Poppy's strong suggestion had now converted into a command.

Obediently, Oscar steered the gigantic car over a sidewalk, through the downpour, into the nearest driveway. Poppy jumped out of the car and ran to the driver's side, while Oscar sidled his large body into Poppy's place. Ivy leaned back with a great sigh and fondled the nap of the soft upholstery.

Expertly, Poppy maneuvered the Cadillac back into the moving traffic, keeping the pace slow.

"I believe that big sister of mine is right. This could be the biggest storm in a hundred years." Oscar slapped his fat thigh like a bass drum. "That's almost as old as the biddy. Ye see, I am the baby of eight children, ten years younger than Eugenia. The gal has still got her instincts, but, I tell ye, I am in possession of my senses. Sister cannot hear, cannot smell, cannot taste. Her seeing is all right, but when the gal goes to singing, she'd like to make us all deaf."

"Where are the others?" Poppy inquired.

"The others? What others?" Oscar repeated the questions, having lost the drift of the conversation.

"Your other brothers and sisters?"

"Ah, the lassies, all gals, they were. Seven sisters like the stars themselves, and I was the youngest, the biggest, and the only boy. They spoiled me rotten. All sisters, and all dead, except for Eugenia. She doesn't like to spoil me so much anymore." Oscar's grin reached from ear to ear. "She likes to shout at me instead."

The water fell from the sky by the bucketful. Dozens of head-lights and tail-lights flashed along the boulevard, but any visible sign of buildings had slipped away, hidden by the grey wash of rain.

Finally, Poppy came to the park's spacious entrance and wound through the groves of poplars, cypress, and eucalyptus. Under the trees they were protected, and the beat of the insistent raindrops subsided.

"Ye do pretty well with this pet," Oscar said, his abdomen against the dashboard.

"Pet?" Poppy was bewildered. "You mean the car?"

"Surely, it is a car, a motorized vehicle with a combustion engine, featuring eight cylinders and hundreds of horsepower, but I like to call it my pet or baby or buggy, my pony, chassis, lassie, sweetie, whatever. Did ye ever drive a car as big as this buffalo?"

Poppy cut the ignition and for a moment sat peacefully listening to the rain whip and rage around them. "Yes, I have driven a car this big," he finally answered, "many times."

"When, Poppy?" Ivy asked with disbelief. She had only seen him in an old red van, and it was difficult to picture her father in his ragged clothes with unbrushed hair and an unshaved beard inside a luxurious Cadillac.

"A long time ago, when I was a boy in New York," Poppy said matter-of-factly. "My father collected Cadillacs."

"What a curious thing to collect. Imagine, taking a fancy to such large pets. Like big game hunting, I suppose. But these need constant attention. They have to be polished and cleaned, washed and rubbed. Yes, ye have to treat a car as good as a lady." The front seat bulged with Oscar's enormous weight.

"My father was an odd man," Poppy's tone turned cool and distant, for he rarely spoke of his father. "He had a special garage built, and the Cadillacs he didn't store on the estate, he put in a nearby warehouse."

Oscar removed a cigar from his breast pocket and twirled it between his lips like a baton. "How many of the pets did he own?"

"There were twelve Cadillacs in the collection, and he usually drove a different one every month. After I learned to drive, he let me take out a left-over once in a while."

Although Ivy had heard snatches of stories that described her grandfather's riches, surely he was not so rich as to collect Cadillacs.

Once again Oscar Orr inspected Poppy's unwashed, disheveled, unkempt, and generally poor condition. However, there was no hint in his look that he disbelieved Poppy's story. "I once knew a gent outside of London," Oscar offered, "who collected motor bikes. A bit like ye father, ye might say, but on a smaller scale. Every New Year's Day he opened his garages to the public. There were dozens of splendid motorbikes from Italy, Spain, Germany, America, and, of course, England. Except for an old Triumph model, he never took them out, he didn't. He liked the looks of them, he did. The gent was my second eldest sister's brother-in-law.

Those motor bikes were worth a fortune then."

"Must be worth a hundred fortunes now," Poppy said.

"Worth nothing now," Oscar said sadly. "Bombed to bits in the war. He died too, the poor chap, out in his barn. Obliterated along with the motor bikes."

Poppy shook his head in sympathy, and Oscar muttered "poor chap" a few more times. There was silence, except for the rain. Poppy listened for a break in the unrelenting storm, but there was none.

"When the weather starts to let up, Mr. Orr, we'll get out of your way," Poppy said.

"To go where?" Oscar looked around for nearby houses.

"We've got some of our things stored in there," Poppy waved towards the woods.

"In where?" Except for the park's outhouse, there was no dwelling in sight.

"In the woods," Ivy explained. "That's where we live now."

"Ye things are bound to be ruined in this rain," Oscar spoke as if it were perfectly natural to live in the woods, as if it were perfectly acceptable to use a tree as a closet.

"You're probably right about that," Poppy answered. "If not ruined, at least soaked."

Ivy suddenly realized how awful it would be once they got out of the car. After they found their drenched bedding, no doubt they too would be wet to the bone.

"Maybe Mr. Orr could drive us downtown to the shelter where we eat breakfast," Ivy suggested.

"Don't you think the Orr's have done quite enough for one day?"

"It's getting on towards lunch," Oscar said, "and sister has a fit to rival this storm if I'm gone too long. But I hate to leave ye anywhere out in this weather."

"We hate to be left too," Ivy piped up.

"Ivy, when did you start thinking I couldn't take care of you?" Poppy sternly asked. "Now we are going to get out of the car, thank Mr. Orr, and let him get back home to his sister and his lunch."

A torrent of water burst through the trees overhead. The windows were clouded, and it was impossible to distinguish any object on the other side of the glass.

"Aren't you afraid to drive alone in this weather, Mr. Orr?" Ivy questioned. "Aren't you worried about seeing the road?"

"Always worried about seeing the road," Oscar smiled sweetly. "Ye know, I got my senses where the old gal doesn't have hers, but I admit to ye, it is sometimes hard to see."

The rain struck the car like a swarm of giant bees.

"Mr. Poppy," Oscar suggested, "why don't ye go find ye things? We'll put them in the trunk of the pet here, and then ye can drive yeself over to the place where ye are going." Oscar consulted his watch. "I have fifty minutes before sister takes it into her noggin' to get the Highway Patrol. But ye know, once I get going, it doesn't take me long to get anywhere. So what do ye say?"

"I say that's a terrific idea," Ivy answered. "Just terrific, Mr. Orr."

From the floor of the back seat, Oscar pulled up a beach umbrella and handed it over, "I am a big man and always have to have things custom-made. I can't go into a store like my fellow human beings and buy shoes. I have to curl up like a worm to sleep in a hotel. My head is too big for most hats. Mister Poppy, I do not like to get my own noggin' wet and that is why I have such a large umbrella. Go on, ye take it."

As Poppy opened the car door, he gingerly raised the lever on the umbrella's handle. Its sections were colored like a beach ball, and it covered Poppy like a one-man tent. Three men his size could have snuggled under it.

"Go on, go on," Oscar waved to Poppy, consulting his watch again.

From under the shadow of the umbrella, Poppy stared at Ivy in the back of the huge Cadillac and studied Oscar in the front, leaning against the dash. Poppy was accustomed to constantly protecting Ivy in the streets and shelters, in situations where they found themselves among strangers. He had trained her to look for signs that someone might suddenly go crazy or get violent. He had taught her to avoid people with spooky looks in their eye. Once at a shelter on Army Street, a man had tried to throw a knife at a group of small children, and Poppy had been the one to stop him.

Ivy too had trained herself to look at who was coming towards her, who was following from behind. Since they had lived on the streets, she had become mistrustful. Poppy said it was unfortunate how some people turned out, but wishing it wasn't so wouldn't make them go away. He told Ivy that being careful was the first step to becoming wise.

"Get off with ye, Mister Poppy, before sister has a fit."

Poppy, however, was having second thoughts. Who were these strange Orr's, offering them food, the use of their car, and a giant umbrella? Who were they, and what did they want from him and Ivy?

Chapter 8

"IVY IS COMING WITH ME," POPPY'S VOICE ECHOED FROM UNDER THE umbrella.

"Ye don't want to be dragging ye little girl into this storm, do ye?" Oscar asked.

"Ivy has to come with me. Right now." Poppy stiffened an angry index finger at his daughter and motioned for her to get out of the car.

Ivy frowned as she pulled the collar of her jacket up around her neck and reluctantly opened the back door.

"It might take us a few minutes to find everything," Poppy explained.

"Go on, take ye time. If sister removes my head when I get home, I can tell her it was all ye fault."

Under the giant umbrella it was perfectly dry, and Ivy cuddled against her father's arm. He leaned down and gave her a kiss on the top of her head where traces of blood had turned purple and stiff like grape-colored straw.

"Why couldn't I stay in the car with Mr. Orr?"

"We don't know these people, Ivy." Poppy said with a withering look. "I can't leave you with a stranger."

"I wouldn't mind," Ivy voiced sincerely. "He's nice, and his sister is too."

Poppy thought that the Orr's appeared decent enough, but lately he had become suspicious of everyone. He could hardly look a stranger in the eye, and when a stranger spoke to him, he generally didn't respond. Living out in the streets, eating at shelters, trying to find work, all these experiences had left a bad, bitter taste in his mouth. He was not only growing suspicious, but afraid. He was afraid that the world had turned its back on him forever.

"It would have been all right if I had stayed with Mr. Orr," Ivy repeated.

Poppy studied his daughter's puzzled face. Although there was sadness in it, there was also still trust. Despite losing their home, she had managed to keep faith that someone would help them, that something would come along.

The chalky-green eucalyptus leaves swirled in puddles of brown water along the path. Rivulets, created by the rain, crisscrossed the hillsides like a nexus of veins. The park's small creeks swelled and overflowed in bubbling torrents.

Carefully, Poppy and Ivy wended their way down the paved footpath, then stepped cautiously across a soggy field to the ravine where they had left their things. Poppy spotted the sleeping bags right away, unrolled like two sleek seals thrown across the rocks, sagging under the weight of the water.

"Ivy," he suggested, "you stay here under the umbrella, while I go collect the things."

Poppy dashed into the storm, returning every few moments with another item. A saucepan, a can opener, a plastic bowl. They piled up beneath the umbrella. A canteen, a ruined book, a box of tools, Ivy's Swiss Army knife, a useless pack of matches, a couple of soaked sweaters. It was a disaster.

Poppy was in despair. It would take days for their things to dry, and already in these few short minutes the rain had soaked his head and jacket. His shoes squeaked when he walked.

"I think that's enough for now."

Ivy looked at the mound of muddy, wet articles.

"Did you find my rocks, Poppy?"

"Rocks?"

Ivy peered at the rain hitting the side of the hill.

"My rocks," she said insistently.

"Ivy, there are a lot of rocks out there. I didn't see any that had your name on it."

"Poppy, you know my rocks!" Ivy pleaded. "My black rocks! My obsidian rocks! The ones from Mount Shasta, the ones I've had since I was a little girl."

"Ivy, you'll have to forget about those rocks for today."

"I can't leave without them."

"What do you mean?"

"I have got to have those rocks," she begged.

"You'll do exactly as I say," Poppy ordered. "Those rocks could have bounced anywhere, or the rain could have washed them deep into the gully. Now pick up those things and get back to the car."

At that moment, Ivy dropped the handle of the umbrella and took off into the storm.

"Ivy! Ivy!" Poppy yelled frantically, "Come back here right now."

She slipped and slid on the muddy slope of the ravine. In no time, she was soaked through. With her shoes she kicked the fallen branches. With her hands she lifted piles of drenched leaves. She found three candles, the dented lid of a saucepan, and a pair of pink socks, but the obsidian rocks were nowhere in sight.

"Ivy! Ivy!" Poppy shouted above the din of the rain.

Ivy examined the side of the hill, trying to locate the exact spot where she fell. It was impossible. The rain had changed the terrain. The gale winds blew around her, water poured down her jacket onto her back, and her hair clung to the sides of her face in thick clumps.

"Hopeless," she said, her fingers digging furiously into the muddy ground. "It's all hopeless." Then she began to cry. The cries rose to sobs, as she wished she had a mother, wished she had a house, wished she and Poppy belonged somewhere. Anywhere.

When Poppy reached Ivy's side, her tears were as thick as the rain. He tugged on her arms, trying to lift and hug her, but she was no longer a little girl. Rather than raising her off the ground, he could only cradle her against his chest.

Ivy swallowed a sob and blinked back the tears. If she had a nice soft bed to throw herself on, a room to lock herself in, a cozy, dry lap to crawl onto, she might have continued to cry, but none of those luxuries were in sight. Poppy was right. She would have to stop thinking about her rocks. She would have to help him. They would have to wait and come back after the storm.

"We won't be able to carry everything," he said, wearily lifting the soggy sleeping bags. "I'll take these." He pointed to the box of tools and added, "You can carry that."

Ivy scanned their junky belongings. It was everything they had in the world, and it was the biggest mess she had ever seen.

Poppy heaved the bags over his shoulder like sacks of potatoes, and Ivy held the umbrella and tool box. Solemnly, they walked through the forest toward Mr. Orr's car.

When they arrived at the parking lot, the powder-blue Cadillac was nowhere in sight. In fact, there were no vehicles anywhere, and the full force of the storm had resumed.

"Now that is what I call friendly, leaving us here to rot," Poppy threw the heavy cargo onto the pavement. Curses poured hotly out of his mouth like machine-gun fire. "I guess we're on our own again, princess," he said, balancing the umbrella over their heads, "with this to keep us dry."

"He was such a nice man," Ivy said with conviction.

"So it seemed," Poppy sneered.

Ivy looked in all directions. There were no signs of people — only rain, trees, rocks, and empty parking spaces.

"Maybe we scared him," Ivy mused, thinking they were frightfully different from other people.

Poppy always said he was different because he was an artist. He told Ivy that he was raising her to be a little different too. "It isn't a crime," he said. "In fact, it's a tradition for artists to be different."

Ivy knew these opinions of her father and accepted his funny clothes and long hair. But recently when she caught glimpses of her own face in a mirror, she looked wild. She didn't want to resemble the homeless people whom she saw around her. She didn't want to be that different.

"Scared Oscar Orr?" Poppy laughed. "He about scared me to my grave with his driving."

Ivy laughed too, for Mr. Orr had twice slipped off the road and almost crashed into another car.

"Maybe you're right, princess," Poppy's voice grew thoughtful. "Maybe we did scare him. Everyone is so frightened of everything these days. Maybe he remembered that we were strangers and that he had already done enough to help us."

Ivy silently vowed that if she ever had the chance to help someone, she would not stop in the middle. She wouldn't leave a girl and her father stranded in an empty parking lot in a storm. She hated Mr. Orr and Miss Orr for taking them in, feeding them delicious things, driving them in their comfortable car, and then deserting them like stray cats. The Orr's would never treat an animal like that, and they'd probably be kinder to a lost dog than a person.

At that moment, the voluptuous fender of an old powder-blue Cadillac rounded the corner of the drive and bumped into the curb.

"Here ye go," Oscar threw Poppy the keys out the window.

Poppy opened the trunk, dumped the wet articles on top of the spare tire, lowered the umbrella, and got into the car. Soaked and chilled, he and Ivy sat shivering in silence for a few moments. Then Poppy turned the car around and drove slowly through the park in the direction of downtown San Francisco. Soon they were traveling past the Opera House and Symphony Hall.

"I hope ye weren't scared that I left ye," Mr. Orr said softly. "I thought it best to call the sister and tell her not to worry. Now where are we going?"

They passed scores of homeless people, sheltered from the rain in the wide doorways of office buildings, huddled at bus stops and under awnings.

"That's our house," Ivy said as they crossed Market Street.

"That was our house," Poppy corrected her.

From the car Ivy could see her old room through the large upper window. Pots of begonias were visible through the glass. "Poppy tried to get work, but there wasn't any. They cut off our phone and threw us out."

"Ivy, hush," Poppy ordered.

"But that wasn't fair after we paid to fix up the place so pretty. There was a big swing in the living room, and Poppy painted birds on the ceiling of my room."

"That is hard luck for ye," Mr. Orr sympathized.

"Rotten luck is half of what it is," Poppy said grimly. "We'll get off in front of that church over there."

Under the facade of the Mission-style church, a cluster of homeless men stood wet and forlorn. On the side of an ugly attached concrete building a sign read —

BUENA VISTA CENTER FOR THE UNFORTUNATE

"Let me talk to my sister," Oscar said, sliding over to the driver's seat. "There might be work ye can do for us at the house."

"Thank you, Mr. Orr," Ivy exclaimed.

"Keep the umbrella," Oscar offered. "Ye might find a need for it in this weather."

Poppy nodded shyly, took the grand umbrella, shook the drops from its frame, and opened it above them. On such a gloomy day its brightness stood out like the sun. Mr. Orr moved the car unsteadily away from the curb, and Ivy and Poppy ran in the pouring rain toward the shelter.

Chapter 9

A T THE *BUENA VISTA CENTER FOR THE UNFORTUNATE*, breakfast was served between seven and eight in the morning, dinner between five and six at night. During the hours in between, the shelter's sleeping areas were closed and only opened after the dinner dishes were cleared. Fifty foam mats were then distributed on a first-come first-served basis. The recipients of the mats covered the hard wooden floor of a recreation hall where the windows were permanently closed, and the tubular fluorescent lights glared all night long. Ivy and Poppy had passed only one night in the large, overheated room with five dozen wheezing, snoring creatures.

"Once was enough," Poppy said, for the mats were filled with dirty, disgruntled men. These men were not only homeless but often insane. Poppy said he would rather sleep outside, and Ivy agreed.

Although the spacious meeting and eating halls were closed during the day, a small office remained open. There a desk and phone were available for the homeless who might call to find work, and housing, or the doctors and lawyers who worked for free or low fees. The shelter also permitted its telephone number and address to be used, and so messages and letters for the homeless were often posted on a board outside the office door.

The place smelled like a combination of sweat, disinfectant, and boiled vegetables. Ivy hated it. In fact, she had come to hate everything about the BUENA VISTA CENTER FOR THE UNFORTUNATE. Not only the odor, but the food, the over-crowded bathrooms, the hopeless human shapes.

Poppy and Ivy were drenched to the bone when they arrived, and the first thing they did was check the corner crammed with cardboard boxes of donated clothes.

"We have to get out of our wet things or we'll catch something worse than pneumonia," Poppy said.

He found an old pair of overalls, a shirt, and a cardigan wool sweater in the men's donations, but Ivy only turned up flimsy blouses and wrinkled mini-skirts.

"There's nothing for me to wear," she cried.

"Let me look," Poppy said, pulling out the same tattered clothes Ivy had rejected moments before. Then from the men's box, he produced a pair of jeans and a warm, flannel shirt. "These will have to do," he said.

At the bathroom sink Ivy met her friend Clarisse. It was said Clarisse had lost her husband several years back, then lost their business in debt to the hospital, then lost their home, and finally was reduced to living in her car. She was almost sixty years old and always wore a stylish, colorful beret. Clarisse told Ivy she couldn't afford to have her hair done or dye out the grey any longer, so she kept it covered all day. She worked in the best department store on Union Square and appeared as if she'd stepped off the train from one of San Francisco's wealthy suburbs. Clarisse used most of her salary to pay off medical bills and hadn't yet saved enough money to rent an apartment.

Clarisse sold scarves, handbags, costume jewelry, gloves, and, of course, hats. Her own large collection included straw, felt, and velvet hats, some dotted with sequins or feathers stuck in the brims. Clarisse's hat collection was the one personal item she had not abandoned in the ups and downs of losing everything else.

Clarisse insisted that Ivy call her Aunt Clarisse. "Kids need as many relatives as they can find these days," she said, "with families so scattered, and children growing up not even knowing their blood relatives."

That was true. Ivy had never met her own grandfather in New York nor any of her mother's family far off in Australia.

Whenever Aunt Clarisse ran into Ivy at the shelter, she always found a little something to give her. She would reach into the bottom of her big plastic purse and bring out a "sample" from the department store — a slender glass vial of perfume or tiny pearls of bath oil. Clarisse showed Ivy and Poppy kindness, and Poppy said that was quite a gift itself, considering what they had all been through to end up homeless and on the streets.

"I couldn't face work today," Aunt Clarisse moaned in front of the mirror. "It's too depressing on a miserable day to watch shoppers buying when none of us has even an extra dime."

Ivy put her hand on Aunt Clarisse's shoulders, and the big woman turned and gave her a hug. "You poor child," Aunt Clarisse exclaimed. "You're all wet."

Clarisse rubbed Ivy's damp neck, removed her soaked shoes, and massaged her entangled hair, tinged pink from the bloody fall. Bending the girl's head under the faucet of the sink, Clarisse lathered the long hair, washed the cut, rinsed out the suds, and patted her head dry.

Ivy did not utter a word, but suddenly in one breath, she burst out, "I fell down a ravine in the woods, but Dice rescued me and took us to his house where Miss Orr fed us donuts and her brother drove us in a fancy old car to fetch our things and drop us here."

"That's quite a day already, Miss Ivy."

"Yes," Ivy heartily agreed.

Despite her mood, Aunt Clarisse began to laugh, fishing into her purse and pulling out a tiny vial of liquid.

"This is a little gift for you." The woman's voice grew hushed, "It isn't cologne, Ivy, and it isn't perfume or ambergris. No indeed, these are Chinese smelling salts."

Ivy looked skeptical, for she didn't know what smelling salts were. "Thank you, Aunt Clarisse, thank you very much," she said in spite of her ignorance.

"I have wanted to give this to you for a long time. I thought it might come in handy."

Ivy examined the smoky grey bottle which resembled carved obsidian, like her precious rocks. She unscrewed the lid and whiffed the minute granulated crystals. The smell almost knocked her out.

"That is strong," Ivy gasped.

"Whenever someone you love is injured or sick, rub it on their forehead," Clarisse instructed. "It will make them strong again. It will cure them."

Ivy dropped the little glass bottle in the deep pocket of her dry jeans.

"Use it wisely," Clarisse warned. "Use it only in an emergency. Use it when nothing else will help."

Outside the bathroom, there was scuffling and shouting. A man was running, and a violent argument was brewing down the hall.

"The natives always get restless in the rain," Clarisse stated with her air of authority. According to Clarisse, everything from personal moods to world events was influenced by the weather.

Ivy peeked out the door to see two grizzled men raising their fists.

"Listen, boys," Poppy said, stepping between them. "You can work this out peacefully."

"Get out of our way," one yelled, aiming his blow unsteadily at Poppy's head.

"You don't have to fight," Poppy reasoned.

It was too late. The old men both swung at their enemy and brought Poppy down by mistake. Poppy hit the floor with a hard, stunning fall.

"Poppy, Poppy!" Ivy rushed out of the bathroom with a shriek.

The old men stared down at Poppy. "It ain't me that hit him," one disclaimed in an alcoholic daze.

"I didn't mean to hit him. I meant to hit you, you fool. His face got in the way is what happened."

Ivy bent frantically over Poppy's limp body, much as he had bent over hers earlier that morning. "Get out of here," she shouted to the old men. "Get away from my Poppy."

"What's all this about?" The shelter manager, Mrs. Sawbuck, shouted from the other end of the hall.

"Ain't nothing, I don't think," one of the drunks shouted back. "Nothing at all."

"Then what is going on here?" Mrs. Sawbuck stood over Poppy's body. "You all know the rules — no fighting, no drinking. Now who started it?"

Both old men pointed to Poppy lying unconscious on the floor, "He did."

"He did not," Ivy protested. "They're lying."

Mrs. Sawbuck looked at all of them, including Ivy, with disgust. No matter what she tried to do to help these people, they behaved like criminals.

"Did anyone here, besides this child, see what happened?"

"We did," the two old men insisted. "He tried to knock both of us out."

"They are liars, and they have been drinking too." Clarisse appeared from behind the bathroom door.

"Shut up, you witch," one old man sneered.

"Ivy," Clarisse whispered, "get out your smelling salts."

"She's cracked in the head, and everyone knows it," the other old man announced.

"I think it's obvious who is cracked around here," Clarisse coolly replied.

"Yeah, that's why she always wears those crazy hats — to cover up the cracks."

"One dribble of crystals," Aunt Clarisse whispered again.

Ivy shook a few grains of the pungent salts onto her finger and touched her father's forehead. Poppy opened his eyes at once. They were clear, calm, and resolved. Hopping up from the floor, he straightened the sleeves of his sweater and scowled angrily at the two geezers.

"You making trouble here?" Mrs. Sawbuck asked Poppy.

"I tell you it was those two," Clarisse said. "They are the trouble makers."

"I am going to forget it this time," Mrs. Sawbuck aimed her forefinger at Poppy, "but one more peep out of you, and you are out of here for good."

Poppy brushed off his backside, touched the lump on the back of his head, and nodded to Clarisse. "Thanks for sticking up for me."

Then grabbing Ivy's hand, their bundle of wet clothes, sleeping gear, and Mr. Orr's umbrella, they walked to the front entrance of the *BUENA VISTA CENTER FOR THE UNFORTUNATE*. Clarisse followed, and the three of them stood under the portico of the church, watching the rain.

Chapter 10

T HE STORM CONTINUED FURIOUSLY, THE RAIN POUNDING THE
streets and buildings of the city throughout the afternoon
and night. The waves on San Francisco Bay were capped
with white foam, and travel advisory warnings had been issued for
small crafts. The cables of the great bridges swayed from the force
of the winds, and owners of houses in the hilly sections of the city
and suburbs worried about the danger of mud slides.

Clarisse invited Poppy and Ivy to stay in her car. "In my most
humble abode," she offered apologetically.

They ate saltine crackers and sardines from a tin, drank water from Aunt Clarisse's canteen. "At least, the roof keeps us dry," she laughed in high spirits to have company despite the cramped quarters.

Poppy agreed. He had come around to good spirits too, and he and Clarisse were reminiscing about their families, fortunes, and recent misfortunes.

"I grew up with money," Poppy said. "Where we lived, everyone had a lot of it."

Ivy's eyes lit up, as she imagined large houses, large parties, large bank accounts.

"That doesn't sound so bad now, does it, dearie?" Clarisse exclaimed.

"It had moments of difficulty like everything else. Most people believe that I should have had no reason to complain, but although it was pretty, homelife was not very happy."

"Did you have people to clean your room, cook for you, drive you around, the way rich folks in the movies do?" Clarisse's eyes danced with fascination.

Ivy listened intently, wishing her childhood had been filled with pretty things and all other manners of pleasures and indulgences.

"My mother died when I was young. Just like poor Ivy's. Nothing can make up for losing your mother," Poppy said soberly.

Ivy had heard stories about her grandmother, Rebecca Bly. It was she whom Ivy favored. They had the same unruly honey-colored hair, similar large frame of bones, and identical green eyes. Rebecca died of a brain tumor when she was twenty-nine, and Poppy was four. Without brothers or sisters, his upbringing had been left to nannies.

"So did you fall out with your father when you were older?" Clarisse asked.

"I think I was born falling out with my father," Poppy said. "When I announced to him that I was leaving home to become an artist, he told me that I was a crazy, misguided, and hopeless individual. He said he hoped never to see me again."

"He couldn't have meant such a thing," Clarisse sighed.

"He always meant everything he said," Poppy assured her, his voice half sad, half bitter.

"I bet he would like you if he knew you now," Ivy piped up.

"Princess," Poppy rested his hand gently on his daughter's shoulder, "he would tell me that I turned out exactly as he predicted — a misguided individual."

"My story isn't very dramatic," Clarisse said. "I wanted to be an actress when I was young. That was my dream, and I knocked around the dance hall scene, singing and tapping. Then I thought to try my luck in Hollywood, but I couldn't take the extremes. Life was either very high or very low, and I decided I needed to be somewhere safe in the middle. I settled down and eventually took care of my family. When my husband up and died on me, I started taking care of myself again." Clarisse glanced around the inside of her shabby car. "I guess I haven't done such a terrific job."

"We're all in a mess these days," Poppy said. "All except Ivy here."

Ivy smiled weakly, for inside she felt like a mess herself — wearing strange clothes, sleeping in strange places, having strange thoughts.

Outside, the rain continued to lash against the car. The wind continued to rock it. Occasionally, lightning illuminated the black sky, and far away Ivy could hear the deep rumble of thunder. It was hard to sleep, hard to think, hard to do anything but wearily search for comfort.

Although Ivy had looked forward to sleeping inside anywhere, even a car, it was the coldest, longest, dampest night of her life. She passed it in the back seat of Clarisse's leaky Ford. She could not get comfortable or warm. She tried to snuggle beneath Poppy's arm, but she was simply too big to find a spot against his body. Meanwhile, curled like a baby in the front with a hat pulled over her head, Clarisse snored through the night.

Morning finally came, and although the rain had subsided, the blustering grey dawn promised another day of storm.

"Good morning," Clarisse peered over to the back seat. "Good morning to you," Poppy and Ivy both groaned.

"Beats the great outdoors," Clarisse said.

"That's for certain," Poppy affirmed. "Thank you, Clarisse, for taking us in."

"Those of us in need have got to help each other. Who else is there to do it for us? I remember years ago my husband and I were driving through Tennessee, and outside Nashville we got a flat tire. Nobody would stop to help us, and so we stood in a cold drizzle, watching dozens of cars whiz by. It didn't look as if anyone in the whole state would ever stop. Of course, eventually someone did. He was a man who had just been released from prison and said he knew what it was like to feel all alone."

"Weren't you afraid of him?" Ivy asked.

"If he had showed us a mean spirit, I would have been afraid, but I could tell he only wanted to help."

"What if he was trying to trick you? What if he was pretending to help when all he wanted to do was rob or harm you?"

"Those thoughts passed through my mind too, Ivy, but sometimes you have to give up your fears and trust people," Aunt Clarisse advised. "It often works out for the best."

"Except when it works out for the worst," Poppy countered, "then watch out. That's how Ivy and I got evicted. I trusted my landlord to give us a break after all the money I put into his place, but he couldn't be budged. So here we are — out in the cold."

From the front side of the car the struts of the spectacular Bay Bridge were visible. Trucks and automobiles crawled across its upper span like brightly colored ants. The towers of San Francisco glittered in the dawn from their night-long shower. Everything shimmered, and the air smelled as if it had been created that very moment.

Poppy pushed open the car door to stretch in the crisp morning air. He kicked the busted tires with frustration and swung his arms angrily towards the sky. What else could he do that he hadn't done? That was the question that burned painfully in his mind.

"It's going to get better, Poppy," Ivy said, kissing the tip of her father's nose. "It's going to get better today." Then a silent, wordless prayer passed through the girl's body. From her toes to her ears, longing and hope coursed in her blood, and she thought, it has to get better soon.

Chapter 11

"I WISH WE COULD DRIVE," IVY WHINED.

"So do I," Clarisse decreed, "but my car hasn't worked since August. At least, we're thankful it hasn't been towed away."

San Francisco was quiet and slick. It felt as if they had the entire city to themselves. The traffic that crowded the bridges and highways had not yet filled the streets south of Market with their commotion and commerce. Glad of the break in the weather, birds sang passionately in the few bare trees. Occasionally, there was the sound from inside an apartment of a baby crying to be fed or a dog barking to be let out. A few diners and coffee shops were open for business. One corner liquor store was already filled with its early morning customers. The homeless and poor crammed the entry-ways of cheap hotels, and a few well-dressed business executives made their way from parking lots towards the tall, glittering build-ings of the financial district.

Since the rain had momentarily abated, the walk to the shelter was a pleasant thirty minutes. Once inside, however, the contrast was obvious — noisy and obnoxious.

"I don't feel like eating," Ivy complained.

"You have to put something in your stomach," Poppy insisted. "You'll get weak if you don't eat. Then you'll get sick, and right now we have nowhere to go if that happens."

Ivy moaned. She was already weak and fatigued from lack of sleep and the cramped, damp quarters of Clarisse's car. The thought of food made her insides turn over.

In the dining hall boxes of dry cereal stood open on a stainless steel table. Plastic containers of milk, bunches of under-ripe bananas, a five-pound bag of sugar, paper cups, and flimsy plastic spoons were scattered across its top. Men, women, and children pushed and shoved to get at the food.

"Don't make me eat," Ivy begged, but Poppy grabbed her by the jacket and pushed her harshly towards the crowd.

He was in no mood for her foolishness. "You'll eat now, young lady, because we don't know when you'll eat again."

As Poppy pushed, Ivy pulled. Finally, by using all her strength, she broke away from him, ran out of the dining hall and into the ladies' room where she was determined to wait until the breakfast hour was over, and the food had been cleared away.

Outside the bathroom door Poppy pounded angrily, "Ivy, come out, or I'll come in and get you." His fists shook the frame of the door, and the women in line at the sink were alarmed by the loud shouts.

Ivy cowered in the corner of the room, afraid to answer, afraid to move.

Finally another voice, louder than Poppy's, reverberated into the bathroom. "Aren't you the one I spoke to yesterday about making trouble around here?"

Suddenly Poppy's pounding and shouting ceased.

"What makes you think you can come into this shelter and cause a riot?" Mrs. Sawbuck railed.

"This is not a riot," Poppy answered firmly.

"It sounds like a riot inside my office. It sounds like a riot down the hall. And it sounds like a riot out on the street."

"I'm trying to get my daughter's attention."

"You've gotten everyone else's. I asked you yesterday to leave peacefully, and I'll ask you one more time today. Clear out or I'll call the police."

"I have to get my daughter," Poppy grumbled.

"If you are not out of here in five minutes, I will call the police. Is that clear?"

Ivy could hear the heels of the shelter manager clicking as she returned to the dining hall.

"Ivy," Poppy said softly, "don't make any more trouble than we already have."

Tentatively Ivy peeked through a crack in the door.

"Get your stubborn self out here," Poppy barked.

"Poppy, I'm sorry," Ivy stuttered.

"Too late for sorry."

Their soggy belongings had been left in a corner of the office, and in order to retrieve them, it would be necessary to see Mrs. Sawbuck again.

As Poppy and Ivy slinked past the reception desk, he caught Sawbuck's critical eye. "Listen, I know I was making an awful fuss out there," he blurted out, "but you didn't ask why. You didn't ask me to explain a thing, and yesterday you took the word of two drunks against mine."

Mrs. Sawbuck sunk behind her newspaper. She was not in the mood to discuss the matter.

"It's terrible to be treated like scum," Poppy added, "and when you don't have anything, that's what the world thinks of you."

Mrs. Sawbuck lowered the paper and rose up on her chair like a sea serpent. "Everyday I come here to try to help you people, but it does no good. You are ungrateful, unlawful, perpetually vagrant in every way."

"What makes you think we aren't trying?"

"Because I know your type, mister. I had a husband as smart as you. He tried to worm his way out of every situation, and all his life he was full of nothing but pitiful excuses."

"Don't judge or accuse me. I'm not your husband." Poppy's words had heated up to boiling.

"I told you, mister, if you don't get out of here, I will be forced to call the police."

"What has he done?" Ivy cried. "He hasn't broken any law."

Poppy smiled at Ivy's defiance. He was glad his daughter was a fighter.

"Ivy, let's go." This was a battle they would lose, no matter what they did or what they said. "It's clear we are unwelcome."

"You got that part right, mister." Mrs. Sawbuck folded her newspaper. "Anyway, what's your name, mister?"

"Samuel Poppy Bly, and don't you forget it." Ivy announced proudly. "He is a great artist."

Sawbuck's eyes hardened into two brittle little nuggets, "Got the girl brainwashed into thinking her troublemaker daddy is a great man. What a bunch of claptrap!" Then turning to Ivy, she added, "Listen, he'll disappoint you. Better get used to that right now."

Ivy's anger bounced like a coiled spring from the bottom of her feet to the top of her throat.

"Hold your tongue, Ivy Bly," Poppy ordered.

"What did you want to tell me, you problem child? Looks to me like you're a chip off your old man's block. I can smell problems when they're still in the cradle — babies crying, wailing, squawking. All of them eventually causing nothing but trouble. I can spot the type."

Poppy laid his hand on Ivy's indignant shoulder and nudged her towards the door. But it did no good. Ivy went right ahead and said what she had to say, "You are crazy."

Mrs. Sawbuck's hard eyes turned deep red. She picked up the

telephone book and slung it towards the girl's head. The heavy book made an ugly thud as it hit the wall and slid onto the wooden floor.

Ivy stuck out her tongue and raised up her fists.

"I'll call the police on both of you," the infuriated woman reached for the phone. "Call to put the daddy in jail and the girlie there in care of the state."

"Ivy," Poppy insisted, fearful now himself of Sawbuck's revenge, "we are leaving."

Mrs. Sawbuck tapped her polished fingernails on her desk, watching Poppy lift their damp, useless belongings.

When the phone rang loudly, all three of them jumped.

"BUENA VISTA CENTER FOR THE UNFORTUNATE," Mrs. Sawbuck answered in a composed voice. "Yes, we post messages for our clients. It's a service the shelter provides for the homeless." Her voice then lifted with surprise, "Did you say Mr. Poppy is the party you are trying to contact? Could you spell that, please?"

"This is Mr. Poppy," Ivy pumped her father's arm up and down. "He is standing right here."

"I can take a message for him." The shelter manager stared blankly at Ivy and Poppy, as if they did not exist. "However, we cannot guarantee that he'll receive it. We don't usually know the names of the people who come here, and many who use the facility once never come back a second time."

Poppy reached over and wrenched the telephone receiver out of Sawbuck's hand. "This is the man you're trying to reach. This is Poppy Bly. Who is this?"

Reluctantly, Mrs. Sawbuck slouched back into her chair.

"Pick us up?" Poppy asked eagerly. "Where did you say?"

Ivy's insides fluttered. Who could be calling? What did they want? Why did Poppy thank them?

Poppy hung up the receiver and once more pushed Ivy to the door.

"Aren't you forgetting something?" Mrs. Sawbuck's eyebrows lifted in a sinister arch.

"What's that?" Poppy questioned, inspecting the floor for forgotten belongings.

"An apology from the brat!" Sawbuck pointed a salmon-colored fingernail at Ivy's face.

That was going too far. Ivy thought she would rather face the police than utter a word of apology.

As Poppy hurried Ivy to the front entrance of the shelter. Mrs. Sawbuck shouted after them. "I want an apology from that brat right now or else I am calling the police."

Chapter 12

DOWN THE HALL AND OUT THE FRONT DOOR, IVY AND POPPY could hear Mrs. Sawbuck shouting.

"Do you think she will call the police?" Ivy asked fretfully.

"I don't think so, but something has sent her off her rocker, and there's no telling what a person will do in that state of mind." Poppy smoothed his rumpled hair and stroked his chin. "Some people only feel good when they're acting mean. Give those people a little authority, and they misuse it with a vengeance."

"But she acted as if she hated me," Ivy stammered.

"Princess, she doesn't hate you. She had to blow off at something, and we got in the way." Poppy put his arm around Ivy and pulled her closer.

While father and daughter stood huddled at the curb, Aunt Clarisse exited the *BUENA VISTA CENTER FOR THE*

UNFORTUNATE. Today she didn't look very unfortunate at all with her soiled but expensive English raincoat, slightly worn wool slacks, and high-heeled leather boots — all of which she had scavenged in a rummage box of second-hand clothes.

"Very nice," Poppy whistled through his teeth.

Clarisse lit up from the compliment and adjusted the purple snood atop her head.

"Not too bad for a homeless old lady."

"You look pretty," Ivy stated simply.

"I am trying, my dear." Clarisse said, rubbing at the coffee stains on the pocket of the raincoat. "Give me a high mark for effort, and today I'm going to go sell my heart out." She checked her watch. "Better be getting over to Union Square."

Ivy watched Aunt Clarisse blend into the crowd. She had observed scores of homeless men and women deteriorate under the strain of their condition, but Clarisse was obviously different. In spite of everything, she managed to keep up her best face. Ivy was certain that Aunt Clarisse would have made a great actress, if life had given her the chance.

"I forgot," Clarisse called to Poppy from the corner. "You and Ivy are welcome to spend the day in my car. If it starts to rain, feel free to go up there."

Poppy nodded his appreciation.

"The key is hidden under the large rock behind the left rear tire."

Poppy waved to signal his understanding.

"I don't want to spend the day in Aunt Clarisse's car," Ivy pouted. "I would rather go to the library."

"We aren't spending the day in a car or a library," Poppy announced gleefully. "We're going to work."

Ivy's legs leapt up in a jig. "Poppy," she exclaimed. "How? Who? Where?" All three questions were garbled into one.

But before Poppy could answer, a dented, powder-blue Cadillac ran over the curb and gently nosed a fire hydrant with its front fender before slamming to a stop.

"Mr. Orr," Ivy's hands clapped enthusiastically. She had never been so happy to see someone in her life.

Afraid that Mr. Orr was a fantasy or mirage, Ivy quickly blinked her eyes. Was it true? Or was she still cramped into the back seat of Aunt Clarisse's car, dreaming? Still crouched by the door of the shelter's bathroom, listening to Poppy's angry pounding?

"Ivy," Poppy snapped, "pick up the bags, and let's go."

Inside the car Oscar Orr beamed beneath his snowy moustache and unlit cigar. He appeared happy to see them again, too.

"How was ye night?" Oscar inquired softly.

"Truthfully?" Ivy grumbled.

"In my book there is no reason to speak unless ye are going to tell the truth. Of course, my sister would tell ye differently. She would tell ye that speech is a form of entertainment. I don't go in for that kind of thing myself. I prefer to open my own mouth when I have something to say, instead of babbling on about nothing. She sings to hear her own voice. She says that is how she knows she's alive, and sometimes when I have not spoken all day, she asks me how I know if I am alive. She says all creatures like to express themselves, and that doesn't constantly mean putting forth a philosophical truth." Mr. Orr appraised Ivy's fatigued eyes, sagging mouth, and unbrushed hair. "I hope ye know that ye can answer with the truth."

"Grim," Ivy said.

A long moment of silence passed before Oscar Orr ventured to speak again. "Ye might ask how my night was, if ye don't have anything else to say. I can tell ye it was a bad one, too. We both, that is my sister Eugenia and I, had a ferocious night wondering how we might find ye again. Then as good luck would have it, I called the BUENA VISTA CENTER FOR THE UNFORTUNATE, and ye were standing right by the phone, and I said to my sister, 'Miss Eugenia,' I said, 'we are in good luck,' and she agreed."

The rain threatened to start again at any moment, and the sky was quite dark for the middle of morning. However, Mr. Orr managed to keep the wheels and bumpers off the curbs and other cars. His hand appeared steady, and despite the slippery streets, their journey across the city was remarkably uneventful.

"I might drive a wee fast for most folks, but without a doubt, I usually drive very well. After I dropped ye off yesterday, I thought

I would not get home alive. The storm jittered my nerves. It was shooting down like whale spray. Sister was about to have one of her cows on the front porch, waiting for me. She got soaked to the bone, which in her case, isn't very far, and was wretched all night." Mr. Orr paused and added. "As was I."

"I'm sorry," Ivy sympathized, "that you were miserable." However, there was no way in the world that Mr. Orr's misery could have compared to her own.

Poppy hadn't said a word. He was tired, although hopeful. At last, he might have found work. If he could get a job and save a little money, then he and Ivy might get on their feet again.

"What kind of work?" Poppy turned to Oscar.

"Ye have to talk to my sister about that. She's the one who runs the show," Oscar answered, swinging into the drive, past the mailbox which said ORR and the weathered green copper plaque, set deep in a low stucco wall, engraved with *Tosca*.

This was the first time that Ivy had approached the house from the street, and it was even larger than she remembered. Under its portico waited Miss Eugenia Orr holding Dice by the collar. As soon as the Cadillac came into view, Dice yelped, woofed, ran, and leapt, all at the same time.

"Out here in this weather, are ye?" Oscar gruffly reprimanded his sister. "As if yesterday weren't bad enough? As if we did not think ye were going to ye deathbed? As if the doctor did not want to see ye in his office at eleven this morning? Eugenia," Oscar said with exasperated love, "ye drive a man to despair with your stubbornness."

Eugenia Orr opened her mouth to speak but instead a song flew out. It was Italian and Poppy grinned at their operatic welcome.

"Bambina!" Miss Orr cried out to Ivy. "Bambina!" Then with the help of her cane, she descended the flagstone stairs, singing, "Mister Poppy, ever so glad ye have returned to *Tosca*."

"Woooffff-yappp, woooffff-yappp." Dice ran circles around the reunion, and his series of wooffffing and yapppping were constant as he raced down to the mailbox and back.

Poppy sat shyly in the car, his hands shoved inside his overalls. "I hope I can help out, Miss Orr," he stammered, "but I haven't yet heard what you would like me to do."

"When Eugenia Orr gets an idea in her head, it is impossible to shake it out," her brother explained. "It sticks like a trunk on an elephant and a fin on a fish."

Chapter 13

As Poppy and Ivy jumped out of the car, Miss Orr slid in. "The two of ye can let yeselves in through the back door," she waved. "It's open." With those brief instructions, the car vanished out of the drive.

Dice followed the bedraggled pair onto the back porch, past the stacks of canned goods and boxes of bottled drinks. It had finally started to rain with a dreary constancy, and the dank kitchen smelled of mildew.

"It stinks in here," Ivy wriggled her nose in disgust. The smell was all too familiar from the donation clothes at the shelter.

Scattered on the table and along the counters were dozens of dishes — empty bowls rimmed with hot chocolate and coffee, plates full of donut crumbs, ashtrays of sodden cigar stubs. Dice scurried to and fro while the collection of cats lounged lazily on the floor. Outside, the pale overcast daylight flickered through the dirty film of windows, and the old clock ticked loudly.

"What shall we do?" Ivy asked with bewilderment.

"We'll start by cleaning the kitchen," Poppy suggested, "which might take a week in itself. I could work here for a year and never run out of things to do. The walls are filthy, the windows in disrepair, the yard overgrown, and the roof tiles broken. That only accounts for the small portion of house that we've actually seen."

Following the gong of a timepiece buried in the interior of the house, Dice sped out of the kitchen.

Ivy looked longingly after him. "May I?" She pleaded.

"May you what?" A disgruntled expression crossed Poppy's face. It was irritating not knowing what the Orr's expected of him or what they intended to pay.

"Follow Dice?" Ivy quivered, pointing towards the kitchen door that opened into the rest of the large house.

"All right, but don't stay away too long. After I get organized, I'll need you to help."

Ivy crept out of the kitchen through a dark, unlit hall, into a huge dining room where a table set for twelve, complete with gilded dinner plates, wine and water goblets, heavy silverware, and pink linen napkins, was laid out for a party. In the center of the table was a vase filled with a bouquet of dead flowers. Ivy swept her finger across one of the plates and a thick layer of dust rose in the air.

Next she crossed a foyer into the living room where a baby grand piano commanded one corner, and two overstuffed horsehair sofas filled another. Chairs and music stands were haphazardly placed around the room. Covering the parquet floor was a deep red Persian carpet, littered with magazines and books. As Ivy stepped onto its plush nap, dust lifted in wisps of smoke drifting up to the crystal chandelier above her. Along its swinging ropes of crystal beads, delicate cobwebs linked together an elaborate chandelier of their own. At the far end of the room Ivy spied a glass sun-porch with a large blooming camellia bush in its center. The bush had grown straight through the floor, its roots buckling the Spanish tiles. Ivy's eyes peered into the spacious vestibule where a circular staircase led to the landing on the second floor. There was no sign of Dice.

On the mahogany lid of the piano were dozens of ornately framed photographs. Each pictured a version of a young Eugenia Orr. Sometimes she was costumed, sometimes not, but always her mouth was round and open as if she were singing. The photographs were inscribed with odd-sounding names. "For Eugenia, our rare nightingale," one read. "For the Grandest Dame of Song," said another. Near the piano were plaques and awards, announcing Miss Orr's opera roles in Paris, Milano, Vienna, and New York. The word *Tosca* was scribbled across an oil painting where Miss Orr appeared wrapped in a hooded cloak that barely concealed the folds of a low-cut, full-length green velvet dress. Her painted black hair flowed softly around her face, and her grey-violet eyes stared boldly out at Ivy.

From the second-story landing, Dice bounded down the stairs, tumbling and recovering himself on each step. He stopped at Ivy's feet, thumped his tail on the Persian carpet, and gargled affectionately.

"So this is where you live, Dice?" Ivy stooped over to tickle the dog's ears. "In this magnificent house?"

Dice wiggled his hind quarters, snuggled close to Ivy's feet, cocked his head to one side, laid it over his front paw, and listened attentively.

"My grandfather lives in a big house too," Ivy boasted, "but I'll never get to see it. He doesn't like my father. Poppy never did anything to hurt his father but be himself. Poppy says that shouldn't be a crime, but in his case, it was."

Dice's tail thumped along with the mournful intonations of Ivy's words. Then burrowing his head on top of her shoes, he licked their soles and laces.

"I guess I'll never even know my own grandfather." The girl's voice trembled, and her eyes grew teary. "I never knew my mother either."

"Ivy," Poppy's voice calling from the kitchen sounded a mile away.

Brushing away the tears on her face, Ivy reluctantly retraced her steps past the long French windows, through the foyer and dining room, down the dark hall while Dice followed faithfully behind her.

"After you dry them, stack them on the table." Poppy threw Ivy a dishcloth.

She dried cups, glasses, dinner and salad plates, spoons, cereal and soup bowls, forks, ashtrays, and knives. Then she turned to frying pans, pots, kettles, steamers, saucepans, and lids.

Poppy scrubbed the stove and countertops, handing Ivy a broken broom and rusted dustbin.

"We'll be doing this forever," Ivy complained.

"I wouldn't mind doing something forever, if I could make a few dollars at it."

Ivy's eyebrows wrinkled and frowned. "What if they liked their kitchen the other way?"

"They can't possibly mind someone coming in and cleaning up," Poppy explained. "Everything around here is either dirty or broken. Anyway, what else could they have in mind?"

Ivy could see her father liked the washing, scrubbing, and working. She wished that she didn't feel so lazy. Or that she had been born rich.

"Tell me about grandfather's house."

Poppy sighed a great sigh. "It was a large house like this one, but different too. It was always ship-shape. Someone washed the floors every morning and every night. Gardeners made certain no weed trespassed in the yard, no vine intruded on the white-washed brick." Poppy paused, "It was quite perfect."

Ivy wondered how her father could have left such a perfect spot.

"That's the way it was when I was growing up twenty-five years ago. My father had to make everything perfect. He moved hundred-year old trees around the yard whenever he decided they were more suited for somewhere else. That's the way it was back then, princess, but I have no idea how it is today."

As Ivy listened, her broom collected balls of dust and bushels of crumbs. While she swept, she imagined perfection. "Everything was perfect," he repeated scornfully, "except for me. I was the one and only imperfection that my father tried to hide as best he could. I was only allowed to play in my room or away from the house. When guests came to visit, I was kept out of sight."

"That's awful, Poppy," Ivy said, and a long sigh from Dice concurred.

"It wasn't as bad as it sounds, princess. I don't know if it's a trick of memory, or if children find pleasure in most circumstances. After all, I had toys to play with, volumes of books to read, and a forest to explore. Although I was neglected and ignored, it wasn't so awful after all. There were neighbor boys to roam around with. My nannies seemed to care about me. They made sure I had a bit of affection. Painting saved me. At least, it saved the best part of me."

Mulling over Poppy's words, Ivy considered that perhaps she might someday look back on her own childhood with thoughts of pleasure. Car trips to Mount Shasta, bright nights camping under the stars, hot sand beaches with fancy drip castles and cool blue waves. However, she worried that their homelessness meant that all the wonderful times were over.

"These times might prove to be wonderful too," Poppy said, as if reading her thoughts.

Ivy regarded the broom, the debris, the dirty walls, and grimy windows. Sweeping, cleaning, and dusting were not exactly childhood pleasures.

"I doubt it," she sneered.

"How about breakfast, princess?"

Ivy was instantly famished and regretted that she had ever refused a bowl of cereal at the shelter.

"In the world of the wealthy and elite," Poppy imitated a shrill British butler's accent, "when we ingest eggs at this hour, we call it 'brunch,' a dainty situated between breakfast and lunch. Miss Bly, how does brunch sound?"

Ivy made her voice even shriller. "Melville," she said, calling Poppy by his middle name, "make that brunch, and make it snappy!"

"Yes, Miss Bly, we know what happens when your patience is tried." Poppy's voice rose in a high whine, "Lamentably, the last butler had to be replaced when your temper scrambled him instead of the eggs. Or was it fried?"

Ivy giggled with pleasure at her father's funny voice and silly story.

"Lamentably," Poppy repeated, and although Ivy was ignorant of its meaning, the word grew into a big joke to her. "Lamentably," Poppy said so that Ivy howled with laughter, clutching her middle and rolling off the chair onto the floor.

"As I was saying," Poppy continued, "lamentably, you have hurt one of the feline creatures beneath your feet. Now Miss Bly, raise yourself up and prepare to eat."

Chapter 14

I T WAS NEARLY TRANSFORMED. ALL THE DISHES HAD BEEN WASHED
and dried, the cobwebs removed, the filth wiped away from the
walls, the blinds dusted, and Poppy had even gone out into the
rain to rinse the cakes of dirt from the windows with a hose.
Although the kitchen was badly in need of fresh paint, its cabinets
in disrepair, its china chipped, and its calendar outdated by
decades, all in all, it was now a tidy, bright, and well-ordered room.

Poppy finally sat down to rest, contenting himself to thumb
through old National Geographics. Rather than rest, however, Ivy
and Dice were eager to play and paced restlessly down the hall
between the dining room and kitchen.

"It stopped raining," Ivy announced with anticipation.

"Woooofff," Dice agreed.

Propped at the kitchen table, Poppy did not respond. Rather he
leaned further over the photos of Polynesia. The bright tropical
warmth was inviting, and Poppy was reminded of the French artist,
Paul Gauguin, who abandoned life in France and retired to Tahiti
to paint. There was nothing Poppy wanted more than to retire

from his homeless condition and be transported to a faraway paradise where he could paint.

"It stopped raining," Ivy repeated eagerly.

"So?" The accompanying glare declared that he wanted to be left alone.

"Dice and I want to go out for a little while."

Through the newly cleaned kitchen windows, Poppy examined the sky. "There are plenty of rain clouds up there yet," he concluded, looking at the bank of swollen, purple clouds that rose, billowed, and reformed into threatening shapes. There was no sign that the storm had actually ended, only that it had abated momentarily.

"We won't go far," Ivy's request sounded reasonable, "and we'll be back soon."

Ivy and Dice strolled calmly through the back porch, but once they reached the yard, there were whoops of delight. Finally, they were outdoors and free.

"Isn't it good to be away from that stuffy house?" Ivy asked, clearing her nose of its collection of dust and dirt.

Dice barked agreeably.

Raising her arms to the dark sky, Ivy made windmill motions. "Do you think it will rain?"

Dice cocked his patched head to one side, surveyed the clouds above them, and wagged his tail.

Ivy tried another more complex inquiry, "Is Miss Orr very old?"

Again, Dice cocked his head, this time towards the other side, and once more, wagged his tail.

Absolute proof, Ivy deduced, pleased with herself that she had proven Dice's intelligence. She had plainly asked him three questions, and it appeared obvious that he had distinctly answered each one.

"Let's take a little walk," she suggested, and as if on cue, Dice bounded towards the broken gate.

Ivy followed, and they were soon passing giant trees and clusters of leafy ferns that Ivy vaguely recognized. In no time, Dice had led them into the clearing where she and Poppy had spent several nights. Grey eucalyptus leaves, blown by the storm, lay over the ground. Busy blue jays, and doves as soft as worn flannel, flew in the tree limbs. Ivy sat down on an old rotten log, and Dice snuggled his head against her knee.

"Shall I tell you?" The girl asked thoughtfully.

Dice's black eyes reflected her question with an inquiring look. "Well, shall I?"

The dog rejoined with his tail.

"It's sad," Ivy trembled.

Dice's tail stopped, and he cuddled more closely against her leg.

"My Poppy loved my mother more than anyone in the world before I came along."

Ivy paused looking at Dice's curious face. "Go on," his expression seemed to say.

Ivy reconsidered. Perhaps she wouldn't talk to Dice. Perhaps she wouldn't tell her story. One large drop of rain fell on the tip of her nose, and she thought the sky might burst in grief if she spoke another word.

Ivy rose from the log and walked towards the rocky, deep ravine where she had tumbled. Dice followed her to its edge, and together they peered at the brambles and brush that grew up and down the steep incline. On the far side, Ivy could see more forest and the distant outline of a tall house.

"They met in an elevator, going to the dentist on a rainy day," Ivy resumed. "Isn't that silly, Dice?"

After all, this was the amusing part of the story, and Dice's responsive tail wagged in assent.

"It was storming outside like yesterday. My mother was drenched, and so was Poppy. It was pouring buckets, Dice, and so when they got into the elevator, they dripped little puddles around the floor. Poppy offered my mother his coat, but since it was soaked, she laughed and thought it was a joke."

Dice peeked at the sky where faraway purple clouds had darkened to inky black.

"Lightning and thunder rolled across the town. There were tornado warnings for the entire state. Then as they were riding up to the eleventh floor, the power went out everywhere." Ivy watched the dog to see if her words passed into Dice's brain. He lay perfectly still, entranced by the story. "They were stuck in the dark between the eighth and ninth floors for four hours. By the time the elevator was fixed, Poppy said he loved my mother."

Another large raindrop fell and struck Ivy's cheek. "Isn't it sad?" A healthy gust of wind shook a thousand raindrops from the trees. They brushed across the ground in whispers like the softest broom.

Ivy did not want to recall the terrible part. What happened when she was three years old was an awful mistake that let her mother drive on a washed-out road. That wasn't how it was supposed to be when they constructed the road, when they built the car, or when the winter storm came on suddenly that took away a chunk of hillside.

"My mother died in a car accident," Ivy said quickly, "and a week later Poppy and I carried her ashes to Mount Shasta."

Ivy took a stick and drew a large conical shape in the muddy ground. It was a picture of the volcano Mount Shasta. "See? That's where we brought the urn," Ivy hurried to explain, "but I was too little then to know what dying really meant."

More rain was shaken from the trees, as if the branches and boughs had listened to Ivy's tale, too.

"I took three rocks from the mountain, Dice," Ivy sighed. "Ever since that day I've kept them near me. I've slept with them under my pillow. I've touched and talked to them. Whenever I was unhappy, I've hugged them." Ivy stroked Dice's warm, silky coat. "They were just old rocks," she admitted, "but they were all I had of my mother."

Dice's ears perked up into two alert cones, saying, "Go on, don't be shy. Tell me the rest of the story."

Ivy watched while the wind swept the sky back and forth across the tops of the tall trees.

"The ashes blew away long ago, but every year Poppy and I go to Mount Shasta to tend the place where we put them. Now there are scrubby plants there, sometimes covered with tiny flowers. I picture my mother coming out from behind a large boulder, walking towards me, and saying in a clear voice, 'Ivy, Ivy, I know you have missed me, but here I am. Here I am, all better now.'"

Ivy pictured Mount Shasta rising from the landscape like a single solitary mother — filled with fire and capped in summer with a crown of snow. "At first," she explained to Dice, "Poppy said my mother was like the mountain. Alive, he said, she had been strong and beautiful like Mount Shasta. But then Poppy began to say my mother was the mountain, and I began to get confused."

Here Ivy's voice choked. She could barely remember her mother alive, and the photos of a tall pale woman with long braids looked no more familiar than a kind stranger.

"You understand, don't you, Dice?"

The dog thumped his tail and licked Ivy's hand.

"Can you help me?" The girl's voice quivered. "Can you help me find my mother's rocks?"

Dice was quiet and around them a light grey drizzle fell like mist.

"I lost them when I tumbled. Can you help, Dice? I must find them, and I need your help."

Dice's head moved back and forth, as if he were considering the magnitude of the problem. Ivy grabbed a large branch for poking through the leaves, and Dice rose. She led, and he followed her through the wet underbrush towards the ravine. Behind the curtain of rain, daylight was fading.

"That's where I slipped," Ivy pointed, "and over there is where the rocks probably fell."

Ivy began her descent down the hill, slipping, sliding, and dragging her branch behind her. Dice slid too. Soon they were toppling towards the bottom where they both landed in a single pile.

Ivy looked at the slick hillside. Her pants were muddy, her left cheek scratched. "How shall we ever get back up?"

Dice panted at her feet, his white spots coated with brown mud, his left ear nicked. His tongue hung loose, but his eyes were sharply focused on a pile of loose twigs. He stuck his nose like a compass into the dirt and barked loudly once, as if to say, "There."

Ivy looked and saw three shiny black obsidian rocks, clinging to each other like magnets.

"Dice," she squealed, picking up the precious objects and holding them in her hand. "It's my mother."

Chapter 15

"THANK YOU, DICE," IVY SAID, RUBBING HIS NOSE AND massaging his ears and back. "Thank you so very much."

Fervently, Ivy clutched the black rocks between her curled fingers. The cool, smooth objects calmed her, despite the cold rain, the sticky mud, and the steep incline above. They sang out to her and connected her back to the world where she could remember belonging. Once there had been a house to live in. Once there had been a few dollars to spend. Once, despite Poppy's unusual style of homemaking, at least there had been one. Ivy put the rocks securely into her pocket, vowing that they would never be lost again.

The grey sheen of sky had been replaced with something darker and more opaque. Light drizzle turned to steady rain, and as predicted, the storm now threatened to return in full force.

Ivy searched for sturdy branches, settling on one as tall as her waist and thick as two wrists. Using it like a crutch, she hobbled a few feet up the hill. However, for every step forward, she slipped back two. Rivulets of water ran everywhere, and the force of the wind was against her. The bottom of her shoes were slippery, and it proved impossible to grip the muddied sides of the steep bank.

Dice cleverly placed Ivy's branch between his teeth and clamped down, pulling and yanking, while the girl held on. Slowly, they managed to climb halfway to the top, but Ivy lost her grip and slid back to the bottom.

"It's not going to work," she shouted up to Dice.

Slipping down the hill with canine determination, Dice dragged the end of Ivy's stick and shoved it back into her hands. They tried his ingenious method a second time, but once again Ivy fell. She was soaked and miserable.

"We'll have to go out another way," she called to Dice. He stood faithfully holding the stick, waiting for her to grab its other end.

Ivy considered the alternate exits. If they headed to the southern edge of the park and the boulevard, they would have to cross a wide creek which was sure to have swelled dangerously from the rain. Then once on surface streets, she was unsure how to find the Orr's house. The western end of the park was bordered by San Francisco Bay, and in this storm its choppy white-capped waves would make it too dangerous to skirt along the boulders. Heading north, they would find the same parking lot Oscar Orr had driven her and Poppy to, but it opened directly onto a highway, where walking was forbidden.

Turning her gaze east, she decided that this side of the ravine was the safest route out. Somehow she would have to scramble to its top. Ivy fingered the rocks inside her pockets. Surely, they could provide her with a bit of inspiration and a dose of courage.

Common sense told her to remove her shoes and to run barefoot up the side of the hill, but after several attempts, that too proved futile.

"Dice, it's no use," she sighed. "We came down here, but now we cannot get out. At least, I can't."

"Whoooff-ooffff," Dice implored, as if to say, "you can do it. I am merely a dog, but I know you can do it."

Ivy shook her head. It was obvious that she could not make it up that slithery bank in the rain. "It doesn't really matter, Dice, because you found mother's rocks."

Dice got the message. He stopped trying to hand Ivy the large stick. Dog and girl stood quietly staring at each other, one waiting for the other to figure a way out of their dilemma.

Despite the lateness of the hour, the volume of raindrops, and the future consequences of Poppy's anger, with Dice's help, Ivy had set out and accomplished what was almost the impossible. The dog had found three pieces of an ancient mineral buried under the debris of the fiercest storm of the year.

Now it was her responsibility to get them back home.

Across the way a deer peeked from behind a sycamore trunk. Its cautious eye met Ivy's and paused. Recently, she had noticed all kinds of animals in the parks. Not only the occasional deer, but curious raccoons who rummaged through their belongings while they slept; chattering squirrels who scampered on the limbs of trees; lumbering possums; and the odorous evidence of skunk.

Dice raised his nose and roared his loudest dog roar.

"No, Dice," Ivy admonished, but the deer had already leapt into the obscurity of the trees.

"I'm your best friend now," Dice's possessive look seemed to say.

"Of course," Ivy scratched the little dog's ears, "you're the best friend I've ever had."

No sooner had the words escaped her lips, than an outburst of violent syllables exploded in the air above them.

"Ivy Elizabeth Katherine Bly" echoed like a bomb.

The girl cringed.

"Ivy Elizabeth Katherine Bly," the voice cried out again, each syllable simulating the ra-tat-tat of a machine gun.

It was Poppy. There was no doubt about that, and from the sound of his voice, it was probable that he was mad enough to discharge a rocket.

Dice shook at Ivy's knee.

When "Ivy Elizabeth Katherine Bly" sounded for the third time, Ivy covered her head with her hands and prepared for total annihilation.

"Yes?" Her answer barely rose above a whisper.

"Are you down there?" Poppy screamed above the din of the rain.

"Yes," Ivy's lips twitched with cold and fright.

"Are you all right?" There was a note of concern in her father's voice.

"Yes," Ivy crouched into a small ball, and Dice buried his head under her jacket.

"You're not hurt?" Poppy peered down the ravine.

"No, not at all," Ivy assured him.

"Then what in the heck are you doing down there?"

Ivy stared at the hillside. She could only see the broad curves of Mr. Orr's large umbrella.

"I was looking for something," she answered, part fearful, part sly.

"In this weather?" Her father stammered in dismay.

"I was looking for something important."

"I don't want to hear your sorry excuses," Poppy retorted. "I've been out looking for something important too, and that is you," he yelled. "Out in this rain, crazed with worry, terrified that something terrible had happened, that you were desperately lost and couldn't find your way back before dark. Do you know what a scare you've given me? And not only me, by the way. The Orr's are sick about Dice, as well as you. They insisted that we call the police, but I persuaded them to let me try to find you first. Do you only think of yourself, Ivy? Do you only think of what you want to do without a fleeting thought for others?"

Ivy was mute, her tongue as thick as a wad of cotton, her eyes burning with chill. Where did he think she was? At a school picnic on a sunny day? No, she was cold, wet, discouraged, disgruntled, and stuck in a hole at the bottom of a ravine. She refused to answer her father's insulting questions.

"Answer me, Ivy." The edict resounded from the top of the ravine.

"No, Poppy," she yelled back peevishly.

"Let's get back to the Orr's house now," he ordered, but there was no love or sympathy in that voice.

"I can't," she yelled out coldly, refusing to plead for help.

"Ivy, I am sick as a man can be of your foolishness. Yesterday you ran off into the rain looking for your blasted rocks. This morning you locked yourself in a bathroom. I have had enough. Now get up here this minute."

Instead of Ivy, Dice's fierce little legs tore up the hill, back-slid once, and finally reached the top.

"Good dog," Ivy overheard her father say. That was typical. He would be kind to an animal, but not to his own flesh-and-blood daughter.

"Next," he prompted.

"I told you that I cannot."

"What is that supposed to mean?"

Ivy wondered if Poppy had turned simple on her, if the past two days out in the rain had squashed his intelligence into putty. "I'm stuck," she confessed.

Poppy sighed, finally comprehending the dilemma. Then without another word, he slid, cursed, and tumbled, as she had before him, and landed in a heap at her feet.

"It's slippery," she remarked quietly.

"Yes, I guess it is," he admitted, inspecting the layer of mud on the soles of his shoes.

Dice moaned with displeasure from the top of the incline. Now there were two of them at the bottom. In an instant, he had joined them, cocking his head and thumping his tail as if to say, "This is a very fine mess we're in."

Chapter 16

"MY FATHER CAN DO MOST ANYTHING," WAS IVY'S VIEW UNTIL recently — to be precise, up to their condition of home-lessness. Before their fatal eviction, she had watched her father admirably cobble together sufficient necessities and an occa-sional luxury to make life both secure and fun. Poppy said it was possible to live decently without being greedy, and he was proud to be a modestly successful artist.

During the past few months, however, Ivy had painfully wit-
nessed their losing almost everything. She had waited for her
father to come up with solutions to their problems, but as hard as
he tried, nothing seemed to work. He had failed to find them shelter or secure himself a meager job. It was very disappointing. Ivy's
faith in Poppy's abilities had been shaken, but she didn't only
blame him.

Ivy made a long list of the responsible parties. She blamed the
President of the United States, her mother's death, her grandfather's wealth, Poppy's unconventional appearance, but most of all,
she blamed herself. Now that his capabilities had proven inade-
quate, she believed that she should be able to step in and make it
better. With her good sense and stubborn attitude, she ought to be
able to fix whatever it was Poppy could not.

"It is a fine mess," Poppy's eyes agreed with Dice, scanning the
steep bank. He lunged upward, extending the umbrella for balance
like a tightrope-walker, but again, cursed, slid, and tumbled.

"What in heaven's name could have brought you back to such
a forsaken place in this weather?"

Ivy pulled the three rocks out of her pocket and cupped them
in her palm. They glistened under the raindrops.

"These," she said solemnly.

Poppy needed no explanation. He knew perfectly well where
those rocks came from, and what they had meant all these years to
a little girl without a mother.

"I guess they aren't going to get us out here," he concluded,
"but maybe this will." Poppy pulled a long coil of hemp rope from
his pocket. "Where's your rope, Ivy?" He looked at her sternly.

She had heard her father say a hundred times, "Never go into
the woods without a knife, a rope, a canteen of water, and a space
blanket."

Ivy hung her head. She had once been a reliable camper. "I did-
n't think I'd need it today," she stuttered.

"Exactly," Poppy said. "That's always the day you do need one."

"Your knife?" He quizzed.

Ivy produced her small red Swiss Army knife. In addition to the one
blunted and two sharp blades, there was a fold-out fork, a corkscrew, and

a plastic toothpick that inserted into the top of the handle.

"Canteen?" Poppy surveyed Ivy's empty shoulder.

"I opened my mouth to the rain when I got thirsty."

"Good answer, but poor excuse."

Ivy smiled. Maybe he wouldn't stay mad long.

"Space blanket?"

The space blanket was an item that folded into something the size of a chewing gum pack but could be spread around a body in cold weather.

"I don't have a space blanket. We haven't had one since December," Ivy reminded him.

"That's right. Well, I guess we'll have to get by without one."

"Get by? Are we going to spend the night here?"

"If we can't get out, I guess we will." Poppy looked up at the darkening sky. "At least, we have Oscar's umbrella."

Ivy and Dice groaned together.

"What about going towards the parking lot?" Ivy inquired.

"Once out of the parking lot, we're on the highway. I'm afraid we'll either get run over or arrested."

"Poppy, we can't stay here the rest of our lives."

"The rest of our lives?" He repeated her words with amused disbelief. "Do you think there's a chance we'll be here that long?"

"It's been a lifetime already," Ivy wailed.

"Oh, that's funny." Poppy threw his neck back so that his head was directly under the umbrella. "That's a real crack-up."

At this raucous display of mirth, Dice's tail wagged in the mud, back and forth like a metronome, as if to say, "Thank goodness, we're laughing again."

"Come on, troopers. Let's get out of here."

Poppy, Ivy, and Dice huddled together and under the protection of the umbrella, moved along a path that headed west towards the parking lot. The way was littered with mounds of leaves, heaps of twigs, twisted vines, and uprooted briars and weeds.

"How in the world did you ever find those rocks in this goop?"

"Dice found them. I told him how important they were to me, and he found them right away."

"What is that supposed to mean?"

"It's simple." Ivy said. "He must speak English because when I explained to him how mother died, how we scattered her ashes, how I had taken the rocks from Mount Shasta, and how they were the only things I had of her, first he listened carefully, next he sniffed around, and then he found them."

"Ummm," Poppy mused, stooping to pet Dice's back. "Miss Orr told me she found him in a garbage can in Paris so he probably speaks French too, n'est-ce pas?"

Dice yelped with excitement, and Poppy gave Ivy a big wink.

"See, Poppy," the girl declared. "He understands you, and he does speak French."

The bedraggled trio walked on, and although the rain inter-mittently fell from the sky in bursts, the canopy of trees and umbrella protected them. In the parking lot was an expanse of empty pavement, one lonely phone booth, and two forlorn bath-rooms.

"I'll call the Orr's and let them know that we're all right."

"Do you have the number?"

"I can call information."

"But the phone is broken," Ivy said, as Poppy inserted a coin.

"So we have one black-and-white dog who is fluent in two lan-guages and a twelve-year old psychic who predicts the working condition of machines." Poppy looked skeptical, as he impatiently tapped the telephone receiver, jiggled the levers, pounded the box with his fist, and finally gave up. "Unfortunately, the girl is right. It doesn't work," he sighed.

"Of course not, or Mr. Orr would have called his sister here yes-terday."

"True," Poppy sighed again.

A ferocious wind swirled leaves, twigs, and branches around in currents that heaved and howled. Ivy clung to Poppy's elbow, while her hand shielded her eyes. Every step was an effort. Poppy lifted Dice to his arms, and they trudged against the wind. Beyond the driveway was the wide dangerous highway. Holding Ivy under one arm, and cradling Dice in the other, Poppy led them onto the nar-row shoulder of the road. The headlights of the speeding cars and trucks blinded them in the dark afternoon, and it appeared as if the traffic were swerving toward them like a serpent's tail. Ivy shut her eyes and let Poppy lead her like a guide-dog. The wind tousled her hair, and the bright stream of lights bored through her eyelids.

Suddenly, the white round flashes of many cars turned to one sustained red strobe. Ivy jumped back with fright as a police car stopped alongside them.

"Car trouble?" The policeman shouted through the din of the traffic and roar of the wind, beckoning Poppy towards him with a long emergency flasher.

"No," Poppy said, forcing himself to sound natural.

"Then how'd you get out here?" The policeman persisted.

"Took a wrong turn," Poppy smiled, hoping the answer would prove satisfactory.

"It's illegal to walk on this highway."

"I didn't know that," Poppy lied.

Ivy knew her father never lied unless he absolutely had to. This must be more serious than it looked.

"Where you coming from then?" The policeman scrutinized their muddy pants and shoes, their soaked jackets, wet hair, and dazed expressions.

"Over there, somewhere." Poppy turned his head and pointed with his tired, pink eyes.

The driver leaned across the seat and asked for Poppy's identification and driver's license.

"See here," Poppy started to get huffy, "we didn't do anything wrong." He added, "At least, we didn't knowingly do anything wrong. We'll get off this road as soon as we can. Walking should not be a crime."

Ivy held her breath. She could sense the lecture brewing on the health benefits of walking, the Constitutional rights of United States citizens to reject the automobile as the primary mode of transportation, the effects of car pollution on the environment, and the hole in the ozone layer.

Fortunately, Poppy decided to hold his tongue on all of the above.

"Can't let you walk another step on this highway. So where's your driver's license?"

"I don't drive," Poppy lied again.

"Are you carrying any i.d. on you? Like credit cards?"

Ivy laughed out loud. Poppy had never had a credit card in his life.

"Library card? Anything to tell us your name?"

"I am quite capable of telling you my name myself."

"I bet you are."

The driver turned to Ivy, covered with mud and scratches. "Who's this?" He asked roughly.

"This is my daughter," Poppy said indignantly.

"Who is this?" He asked Ivy.

"He's my father." She answered decisively.

"Are you sure?" The two policemen asked together.

Poppy knew what that was about. They probably suspected that Ivy was one of the missing children whose face appeared on a milk carton ten years ago. No doubt, they were thinking she had been kidnaped when she was small and could no longer remember who her actual parents were.

"See here," Poppy broke in. "This is ridiculous. If you don't mind now, we would like to get out of this weather."

"Yeah? So where is it you would like to go?"

Poppy frantically combed his brain for the right information. It was useless. He didn't have the Orr's address. He didn't know their phone number.

"We're staying with friends, and I'm afraid I've forgotten the address."

"Yes, this is their dog," Ivy piped in, "and this is their umbrella. They must be worried sick."

"So," the driver exhaled sarcastically, "you took their dog for an afternoon stroll in the worst storm of the century, got lost, ended up on a highway, and can't remember the street address to go back? Is that correct?"

"Sounds like a story to me." The policeman nudged the flasher against Poppy's chest.

"Yeah, yeah," his partner agreed.

"I think you two better come with us."

Chapter 17

"CAN'T HE COME?" IVY IMPLORED, BUT THE POLICE CAR HAD moved away from the highway's shoulder and into the stream of cars. Ivy pressed her head to the rear window and waved wildly at the little dog, but he soon disappeared behind them.

"Raymond and I were out here on a call early yesterday morning," the driver said, pointing his black gloved hand at the policeman in the rider's seat. "Ain't that right, Raymond?"

Raymond nodded.

"Got a 911 call from a bicycle rider. Ain't that right, Raymond? A bicycle rider called in and said a girl had cut open her head and a man who called himself her 'father' was cradling her in his arms. Didn't sound too savory to me."

"That's right," Raymond finally spoke. "Tramped through those woods over there looking for them. Yelled until I lost my voice. I'm still hoarse."

"Both of us got hoarse, looking for those two. Shouting out and nothing answering back. Gave me the creeps, that's what it did."

"Bicyclist said they looked like vagrants, camping out in the park," Raymond explained.

Ivy flinched when she heard the word "vagrant."

"It's illegal to camp in the park." The driver turned to make sure Poppy was listening. "Vagrancy is a crime."

"We looked for over an hour, but we never found them," Raymond swore softly through his teeth. "The bicyclist said the girl's head was bleeding so we couldn't figure. If she was badly hurt, how come she ran away like that? In fact, how could she run away? That's what confused us."

"Thought maybe the big guy finished the girl off and put her body in the bottom of the ravine," the driver continued, "but when we climbed down there to look, all we found were a few old pots and pans, a beat-up suitcase, some old clothes, books, and a couple of kid's things."

"Almost broke my heart to see that girl's sweater lying in the woods," Raymond's voice choked up.

"Yeah." the driver echoed Raymond's concern. "The things people do to kids these days is enough to make me mean, especially in my line of work when I have to see it all."

"People are sick in the head." Raymond reminded his partner.

"Ain't that the truth? I say we got to find the sickos and lock them up for the rest of their days."

"When you two were tramping around, you didn't happen to see a girl hurt back in those woods, did you?" Raymond swung his big sticky-brown eyes towards Ivy. "You ain't that girl, are you?"

Ivy didn't answer. Poppy didn't answer.

Poppy stroked Ivy's hand reassuringly, but there was no reassurance to be had. The very thing they dreaded most had now come to pass. Ivy looked at her father with utter fear. What if they were separated? What if Poppy were put in jail? What if she were taken away?

"Okay," Raymond said, pulling Poppy out of the car by his arm. "You come with me."

Poppy yanked his arm away.

"You ain't gon' find yourself resisting a police officer, are you?" The driver asked with a look that combined cruelty and fatigue. "Better cuff you, if you gon' act like that."

Poppy shook his head sadly and held out his wrists for the handcuffs. It would be best if he could hold his temper and keep the charges to a minimum. So far, all the police had against him was walking along a highway.

"Raymond, you take the girl downstairs. Tell Social Services they better find a temp."

"Temp?" Ivy screeched. "What's a temp? I don't want a temp. I don't want to go downstairs. I don't want to leave my Poppy. Please," Ivy's sobs rose and fell like ocean waves, "please, please, please."

Raymond pulled Ivy's right arm towards the double front doors of the police department, but Ivy pulled back. Her body bucked, her feet sunk into the ground, and she refused to go forward.

"Ivy," Poppy tried to soothe her, "don't make it worse. Just go with them. They won't hurt you."

"Poppy, don't let them take me."

It turned Poppy's heart over to hear his daughter's distress. "They are going to take you, princess," he tried to explain, "and there is nothing I can do. As soon as I get out of this, I'll come get you. That won't be long. Maybe an hour, maybe two. That's all."

"It's not fair," Ivy sobbed until the words spiraled into screams. Then she bit Raymond on the wrist.

"You little witch," he howled.

With the screams, howls, and sobs, five additional policemen ran out the front door to assist. Two held Poppy while Raymond handcuffed Ivy's wrists.

"Be good, princess," were Poppy's last words before he disappeared into the front office and Ivy was dragged downstairs.

"Yeah," Raymond said, "be good or it won't come to any good."

Tears gushed out of Ivy's eyes, and she stumbled several times before they reached the elevator.

"There," Raymond said gruffly, nodding towards a door marked JUVENILES.

Trembling, Ivy managed to walk through the door.

"There," Raymond repeated, indicating one of the straight-backed metal chairs.

Ivy immediately collapsed. All around her was trouble. She could feel it. Thousands of kids in trouble had been taken into this very room and told to sit, told to shut up, told to wait. Then what?

Ivy didn't have a clue. She could recall what she had seen in movies or read in books, but it was too terrible to be real. She tried to make herself stop thinking, stop feeling, stop breathing. She held her breath and waited.

A few seconds passed before Ivy had to gasp for air. She took several short, loud, panicked breaths.

"Something wrong with you, girlie?" Raymond looked at her angrily, "You ain't gon' have a fit on me?"

Ivy shook her head.

"You ain't sick, are you?"

Again, Ivy's head bobbed in despair. After all, she had done nothing wrong. She had never done anything wrong, or at least anything criminal.

She reconsidered. That was untrue. Once, when she was seven years old, she stole a pink plastic pony out of a toy store. When her father found it, he drove fifty miles back to the town so she could return it. He made her take the pony and torn wrapping into the store and tell the clerk what she had done. Ivy had been sobbing that day too, but the clerk had been kind and offered to give Ivy the pony for her honesty. Poppy refused it for her. He said that she had committed a dishonest act and should certainly not be rewarded. Poppy never mentioned another word about it, and Ivy never stole again.

Having assured himself that Ivy was neither epileptic nor asthmatic, Raymond poked his head through a wire cage in the wall and shouted, "Anybody home?"

No response.

Raymond banged the counter.

"Hold it down, Raymond." A policewoman appeared. "You trying to raise the dead?"

"Trying to raise the police department is sometimes tougher. They play dead and then it's hard to tell the difference." Raymond chuckled.

"Okay, save your sarcasm. I get the point. What's the matter?"

Raymond waved the imprint of four teeth on his wrist. "Feel sorry for me, Betty?"

"Break the skin?" The woman asked.

"No, but it hurts like I lost my hand."

"You have no pain threshold, Raymond. Now take me," Betty started to explain.

"I know," Raymond's voice exaggerated his weary disinterest, "men have no pain threshold because they can't have babies."

"That's right."

Betty looked at Ivy for the first time and grinned.

"She doesn't look dangerous to me." Betty returned her attention to Raymond. "You must have done something to frighten her."

Raymond opened his mouth to protest.

"I've told you that you can't bring these kids in here and not explain things to them." She turned back to Ivy and grinned again, "Did he explain anything to you?"

Ivy shook her head.

"See," Betty said, "you frightened her and she bit you. It's pure animal instinct, and it happens to you all the time. So why don't you wise up?"

"She's all yours now, Betty."

"So, what's the charge?"

"No charge."

"I thought so," Betty murmured kindly. "Why the cuffs, big guy?"

"She bit me. I ain't gon' take a chance of her doing that again."

"No, of course not, so you treat her like a common criminal and expect her to behave herself." It was clear that Betty could wrap Raymond's mind around her finger.

"Her so-called 'father' is upstairs," Raymond explained.

"He is my father," Ivy interrupted.

"We picked 'em up on the highway. It's suspicious since yesterday we got a 911 on an accident near the same place. The emergency said a bleeding girl living in the woods with an older man. Maybe her father, maybe not. We tried to find the girl, but she disappeared. Found some artifacts — clothes, toys, a suitcase. Maybe this girl, maybe not. Maybe the guy's running a twelve-year-old harem."

"Sign of foul play?" Betty asked.

"Not really," Raymond had to admit. "But you never know these days with all the perverts walking around."

"And the father? What's with him?" Betty inquired.

"They'll book him for vagrancy, then trace his identity for kidnaping charges. Who knows? I wouldn't be surprised if they don't use him for a few line-ups. He looks like he's been knocking around for a while."

Dejected, Ivy shook her head. Poppy was down on his luck, they were without a home, and now the police suspected him of terrible crimes.

"He is not a criminal," Ivy cried. "He's a wonderful man." Then she added urgently, "He's an artist."

"Sure, sure, I bet he makes real pretty pictures. A con artist, I can believe that. A real con artist."

There didn't seem to be any way to make Raymond understand that she was telling the truth.

Raymond rubbed his wrist with a handkerchief. "Warn the temp that the girl is dangerous."

"Get out of here," Betty teased. "You can't see even one tiny mark so beat it before I tell your boss that you are the biggest baby on the force."

TOSCA

by
Ivy Bly

Chapter 18

THERE, THAT'S MUCH BETTER," SERGEANT BETTY HARMON
said, removing Ivy's handcuffs. "After all, you're not a pris-
oner here."

Ivy rubbed the indentations around her wrists. "He didn't have
to do that."

"You were scared, he was scared. Nobody likes coming to a jail-
house and nobody likes getting bit. I guess that makes you two
even." Sergeant Harmon touched Ivy affectionately. "We need to
take care of you until they let your father go."

Betty led Ivy to a crammed and messy desk. "So?" She
motioned for Ivy to sit down. "Your father's upstairs?"

Ivy glanced around at the high ceilings and scuffed linoleum floor. The blinds on two big windows were partially lowered, and the glass was covered from top to bottom with wire mesh. There were a half-dozen desks, computers, file cabinets, and a mail cubby divided into a dozen boxes. Ivy scanned the slots and spotted HARMON on top. There was a cot in one corner, and a colored photograph of the mayor of San Francisco under a large clock.

"They took him in for walking down a road," Ivy replied hotly. "Is that a crime?"

"Let's call it a problem because it is a problem, if the road happens to be a highway with no sidewalks. It's a serious hazard to motorists and pedestrians like yourself. That makes it a problem."

"Well, Poppy is upstairs because of a problem." When Ivy silently listed the problems and grievances she and Poppy currently had, they were a lot more serious than walking on a highway.

"What's your name?" Sergeant Harmon removed a clipboard from her desk drawer and fastened a form under the clamp.

"Ivy Elizabeth Katherine Bly." Ivy answered proudly. "They call me Ivy."

"Pretty name," Betty muttered.

"Thanks," the girl said automatically.

"Hey, a kid with manners. I don't think I've heard the word 'thanks' in this room for four years."

Ivy smiled. Poppy said that manners were the first thing that showed on a person, and it didn't matter how somebody looked, what they wore, or how much money they had, as long as they showed good manners.

"Pretty smile too, Ivy," the sergeant added. "Your age?"

Ivy relaxed in her chair. Poppy had advised her to cooperate, and she liked this Sergeant Betty Harmon. Okay, she would answer the question.

"Thirteen." That was almost the truth since she had less than six months to go before her next birthday.

"Where do you live?" Betty continued.

That was a stumper. Ivy didn't want the police to think they were homeless or vagrants or bums.

Ivy hesitated, "We are staying with friends."

"So where do the friends live?"

"We can't remember their address." A panic rose inside her. "That's the real problem."

"Is it in San Francisco?" Betty pursued, hiding any surprise at Ivy's lapse of memory.

"Oh, yes," Ivy enthused, "it is in San Francisco, but if you went to their house or spent time in their garden, you'd think you were in a villa in Italy."

"Italy?" Obviously, the sergeant found that surprising.

"Somewhere in southern Europe, but probably Italy. There are roses everywhere, lemon and orange trees too," Ivy bubbled, recalling the magic spell of the Orr's overgrown yard.

"I bet you're a girl with a great imagination! Am I right?"

"It's not my imagination," Ivy squirmed. "Our friends are foreign so their house seems foreign too, and they have a large patch of lawn in the back that no one cares for. Our friends behave as if they're in a storybook, and they haven't changed their calendar since 1952."

"Why would you say Italy?" Sergeant Harmon studied Ivy's face, trying to determine how much truth there was in it. "Have you been to Italy?"

"No," Ivy explained. "But I have a sense about places I've never been. I guess I get it from books and movies." The girl paused, "Poppy always shows me paintings and pictures. He always tells me things."

"So Ivy, you've learned how to 'imagine' things even if you have never actually seen them. Is that right?" The sergeant prodded.

"I guess so," Ivy conceded reluctantly, "but I didn't imagine the house. I didn't imagine our friends. I only imagined that it could be a villa in Italy."

Many young adults, juveniles, who crossed Betty Harmon's path had lots of stories — lots of tales, fibs, and lies. On first instinct, the sergeant had not suspected Ivy as a fibber or liar, but now she started to wonder. "I see your point." Betty contemplated the intelligent, unwashed girl before her.

"I think Miss Orr was an opera star. She has autographed pictures from all over the world, and she's extremely old." Ivy jabbered. "I bet she's almost a hundred."

"Orr?" Betty grabbed the phone book. "Maybe we can call your friends and clear this mess up right away. What's the first name?"

"Eugenia," Ivy faltered, uncertain whether Poppy would want her to mention the Orr's by name, "and her brother is called Oscar."

"O-R-R," Betty scanned the pages. "No E-U-G-E-N-I-A, no O-S-C-A-R, no luck. Too bad." Then, abruptly, she changed the subject, "I bet you like to draw."

"More than anything," Ivy quickly answered. "Poppy's an artist."

"Then draw me a picture of the Orr's house," Betty suggested, offering up pens and a drawing pad.

Ivy went to work, trying to remember the fine details of the old stucco house, the broken tile roof, the crumbling chimneys, the French doors, the wooden shutters. She drew verandas and porticos, a trellis with roses, a crescent-shaped bench curved around the trunk of a large magnolia, and a cracked marble fountain with two white marble doves.

While Ivy drew, Sergeant Harmon used the phone. She gave Ivy's name and age to someone on the other end of the line. When the girl overheard the word "temp," her panic returned.

"What's a temp?" Ivy moaned.

"Temp stands for temporary foster care," Sergeant Harmon explained. "If your father has to spend the night in jail, then we provide you with a place to stay. We take care of you."

Ivy's eyes swelled with tears. "That's not taking care of me," she protested. "Letting Poppy go is taking care of me."

"We're not certain about anything yet," Betty said reassuringly. "They're still questioning your father upstairs. You must be thirsty? And hungry too?"

When Betty returned from the hall, there were chips and sodas for both of them.

"Not too healthy, but it curbs the appetite."

"Thank you," Ivy said gratefully.

"That's two 'thank yous' in one day. Might be setting some kind of record around here, if you don't watch out."

Ivy held her drawing up for Sergeant Harmon. "It's very good," Betty said. "You're a talented girl, do you know that?"

Ivy assented modestly. "Poppy says that talent's not worth much if you don't practice. I'm not too talented when it comes to practicing."

"You'll grow into it," Betty patted Ivy's shoulder. "Is Poppy a good father?" The policewoman asked cautiously, careful not to tread too fast into personal territory.

"Oh, yes!" Ivy stumbled over the words, recalling that everything Poppy did lately seemed to go wrong. "He tries very hard," she added.

"When I say 'good,'" the sergeant explained, "he doesn't hurt you or anything like that?"

"Oh, no!" The girl said fretfully. She remembered how hard Poppy had tried and how ungrateful she had been. It was she who tramped off into the woods to find her rocks and look what had come of it. If only Poppy could get them out of this mess, if only they could be together, she promised herself that she would never be stubborn or foolish again.

"Are you sure he never hurt you?" Betty persisted, knowing the lengths children would go to protect their parents.

"Never," Ivy emphasized adamantly. "Never, never, never. He's the kindest father a girl could want." Ivy made one long sob, "I wish I were with him now."

Sergeant Harmon surveyed Ivy's filthy clothes, tangled hair, and strained eyes. The eyes were swollen from crying, and tears now streaked down her cheeks.

"Here's something," Betty handed Ivy a tissue. "Things will be better soon."

"Thank you," Ivy said again.

"Okay, that's it!" Betty shouted out. "Three times is the millennium record. Tonight you will be entered into either *The Guinness Book of World Records* or *Ripley's Believe It or Not.*"

Ivy smiled as she wiped her face and blew her nose.

"What about your mother?"

The question caught her off-guard, but she answered with the simple truth. "She died when I was little," Ivy said, rolling the three obsidian rocks between her fingers.

"I'm sorry," Sergeant Harmon sympathized.

Ivy thought this woman could be trusted.

"Have you been staying with these friends long?" Betty pointed to the elaborate drawing of the Orr's beautiful house.

"No, not long at all." Ivy said, picking up the pen to flourish the bottom of the drawing with the word *Tosca*.

"What's that mean?"

"It's the name of their house and the name of a famous Italian opera, too. Miss Orr is always singing, even when she's talking." Ivy explained.

"Sounds like an interesting person." Betty jotted a couple of notes on her pad. "Besides the Orr's, Ivy, maybe there is someone else we should call. A relative? A friend? Someone else we can contact for you to stay with in case your father is detained."

"I hope he's not detained," the girl enunciated the odious word. Detained in her mind sounded absolutely final.

"I sincerely hope so too," Betty Harmon concurred, "but I can't make any guarantees."

"Clarisse is my friend," Ivy said.

"Who is Clarisse?"

"She's a woman we know from the shelter."

"Shelter?" Betty's ears perked up.

Ivy hesitated to say more. Maybe Poppy wouldn't want the police to know they had been to shelters. Maybe that would prove they were vagrants.

"What kind of shelter?" The sergeant asked.

Ivy shook her head with embarrassment.

"Does the shelter have a name?" Betty reached for a folder on her desk. "Here's a list of all the shelters in the area. If you can remember the name of the shelter, maybe I can call and ask to speak to your friend Clarisse."

"BUENA VISTA CENTER FOR THE UNFORTUNATE," Ivy blurted out. "It's off Market Street."

"I know exactly where it is." The sergeant reached for the phone. "Why don't I give them a call?"

Ivy recoiled. She wanted nothing to do with that ugly, smelly place. She didn't want to eat or sleep there, or wear its old, stinky clothes. She didn't want to walk its ugly halls, use its crowded bathrooms, or look at its sad, hopeless faces. In fact, she loathed the *BUENA VISTA CENTER FOR THE UNFORTUNATE.* Ivy regretted that she had ever mentioned it by name.

Chapter 19

IT WAS DINNER TIME AT THE SHELTER, AND THE PHONE RANG many times before it was finally answered.

"We have a thirteen-year-old girl here," Sergeant Harmon explained, "who is looking for someone at your shelter."

A dizziness circled Ivy's head, as she listened to the policewoman describe her lonely situation.

"We're trying to contact a woman called Clarisse," Betty continued. "Yes, that's right. C-L-A-R-I-S-S-E. She's about how old?" The sergeant turned to Ivy.

"Sixty," Ivy replied, "and she always wears a hat."

"Late middle age," Betty repeated into the phone. "She's Caucasian and keeps her hair covered with hats. Ivy, do you know Clarisse's last name?"

Ivy shook her head. She didn't know Clarisse's maiden or married name, the name of the department store where she worked, or the street where she parked her car. However, Ivy thought it unwise to tell the sergeant where Clarisse actually lived, for she doubted whether the police would approve of letting her spend the night in a dilapidated automobile.

"The lady in charge has put me on hold," Betty cupped her hand over the receiver. "She says there are hundreds of people who pass daily through the shelter. She seldom knows a client's name. She said it might be difficult to locate this Clarisse by sight, but she'll try."

Ivy's face sunk with distress. She tried to think of someone who might come to help them, anyone who might want to keep her. Poppy's best friend from college resided in Pennsylvania. The neighbor from their old loft had married, moved away, and changed her name. Their cousins in New Mexico lived in a mountain valley without electricity or telephone. Ivy was too ashamed to call school friends. There was a poet in North Beach who played chess with Poppy, but he smelled bad and lived in a hotel. Her mother's family was far away in Australia, and her grandfather was a millionaire who Poppy hadn't spoken to in almost ten years.

Betty dangled the telephone, touching the top of Ivy's head.

"Awwoowowow," the girl yanked back in pain.

"Does your head hurt?"

"It's cut there."

"Let me see," Sergeant Harmon balanced the telephone on her ear and separated the strands of Ivy's hair. "Am I hurting you?"

"It only hurts when you press it."

The sergeant moved a comb carefully across Ivy's scalp, pulling apart sections of her hair, looking for bruises and cuts. Finally, she found a long, jagged abrasion, where the skin had been torn off. The gash was visibly free of dirt, but the raw-looking tissue was purple and indicated infection.

"How did you do that?"

"I fell down."

"Your father didn't want to take you to a doctor?" The sergeant added, "He should have had someone attend to it. It looks like you might have needed stitches."

"No, no, it wasn't bad. It bled a little, but really, it hardly hurt," Ivy stammered. "There wasn't time, you see. We really had to go do something else."

"Yes, I'm still here," Sergeant Harmon turned her attention back to the telephone. "Thank you for getting back to me. I know you must be busy. Yes, let me repeat the information. This is Sergeant Betty Harmon, and we have a young lady here at the police department. No, she wasn't brought in on charges, but her father is being questioned, and we need to find her sleeping quarters for the night. She mentioned a friend named Clarisse who comes to your shelter. Do you think she might be there now?"

Again, the sergeant was put on hold. "She's going to check around for Clarisse," Betty said. "Maybe she's there for dinner."

The news was disappointing. After checking the restroom and dining area, there was no one who fit Clarisse's description.

"If you could keep an eye out for this Clarisse and give me a call if she shows up, I'd really appreciate it. There's a young lady here who would appreciate it, too."

"No Clarisse." Ivy was dejected.

"Here's an excellent idea!" The sergeant exclaimed. "Let's go over to the shelter during dinner hour and look for Clarisse ourselves."

Ivy was immeasurably cheered.

"Let me call upstairs and get someone to come down to JUVE-NILE. I'll check on your father, too. Then we can go over to the shelter while dinner is still being served."

Sergeant Harmon picked up the intercom phone and dialed. "Raymond, how's it going? Everything down here is excellent. Ivy Bly is her name, and she has drawn me an outstanding picture of the house where they are staying." Betty described the details of the picture. "Excuse me, Raymond, but it's more than a house. It's an Italian villa."

Raymond must have made a sarcastic remark because Betty's tone grew very indignant. "I know the difference between a villa and a house, thank you. Hey, I also know what a Tudor is, you ignoramus. So to continue, tell Mr. Bly that his daughter is in good hands."

There was a long, dreadful pause while Raymond told the sergeant how Mr. Bly was doing. With a nod Betty indicated to Ivy that everything was all right upstairs, too.

"Poppy!" Ivy cried into the phone.

"He's doing fine. Isn't he, Raymond? Here, tell the girl."

Betty handed Ivy the phone.

"Yeah, your father's good. He just had a little dinner, and he's doing fine." Raymond's whine was no comfort.

"Can I see him? Please," Ivy cried out again. "Can I see him now?"

"No," Betty and Raymond spoke in unison, "you cannot see him."

Ivy tried to keep herself from crying, but it was a useless effort. The tears poured out, wetting her face and hands and staining the drawing of *Tosca*.

"We're leaving in a few minutes, Raymond." Betty added, "We're driving to the *BUENA VISTA CENTER FOR THE UNFORTUNATE* to see if we can find a Clarisse or anyone else who might know something about them."

Chapter 20

SERGEANT HARMON SPED THROUGH THE STREETS OF SAN Francisco towards the district south of Yerba Buena. It was a fast, thrilling ride, for when Betty grew impatient with the traffic on Van Ness and Market, she turned on the top-whirling police light. The reflection of the cherry-colored beam broadcast in all directions for everything to move out of the way. Ivy watched while streams of cars pulled off to the side, and like royalty, they passed on.

Ivy smiled in silence, dazzled by the importance of their mission. This time around she liked riding in a police car.

The sergeant screeched in front of the shelter, and a collection of loitering men jumped back from the curb. Grumbles went through the crowd. Ivy caught fragments of phrases such as, "Watch out, here comes the cops!" and "Who's in trouble now?"

Inside the shelter, the halls were silent and deserted.

Betty followed Ivy to the office at the far end of the building. The girl trembled, recalling the dismal scene and verbal threats that had transpired there only that morning.

"Sergeant Harmon, I've been expecting you," the woman behind the desk lowered her newspaper and said in a familiar voice.

Ivy's worst apprehension now appeared before her eyes. Mrs. Sawbuck, the demon! Mrs. Sawbuck, the witch! Ivy ducked quickly into the shadow of the door and prayed that she might vanish.

"We do appreciate your cooperation," Betty continued. "It's a small thing, but we might be able to help a very nice girl who at the moment is in a great deal of distress."

"Anything I can do to help," Mrs. Sawbuck replied graciously.

Ivy choked on the sound of that voice.

"You said there was a girl?" Mrs. Sawbuck inquired with a puzzled air.

"Yes, she is searching for someone named Clarisse." Disconcerted, Betty looked around for Ivy. "I brought her here with me," the policewoman stuttered, "but she seems to have disappeared."

"Oh?" Mrs. Sawbuck rose from her chair.

"She was here an instant ago," Sergeant Harmon looked bewildered, "so I can't imagine where she's gone to now."

"Perhaps a bathroom emergency," Mrs. Sawbuck suggested, and the two women followed the hall to the restroom, leaving Ivy hidden between the door and the wall.

Ivy was profoundly discouraged. After all the sergeant's kindness, it was unfortunate that they should come to this place, face to face with Poppy's greatest enemy. How could she have assumed otherwise? Or believed that Sawbuck would have already gone home? Or had an emergency that required her to be away? She had been foolish to let Sergeant Harmon bring her here.

Ivy emerged from the shadow of the door, assessing what to do. The choices were slim. She could either reveal herself or vanish out the back emergency exit. Ivy wondered, waffled, and wavered in the hall. Vanish, yes, she decided, but not before checking the dining area for Clarisse.

Betty and Mrs. Sawbuck were not in sight. Edging her way along the dark wall, Ivy reached the double doors of the room that served as cafeteria. Looking out over the seats of diners, she spotted no berets or fancy hats. A couple of men acknowledged her with a wave, but the dozens of others concentrated steadfastly on their plates. There was little talking and the loudest sounds were the clatter of forks and spoons.

As Ivy turned to go, Mrs. Sawbuck stood blocking the door. "Is this the girl whom we've been frantically looking for?" She shrilled.

Betty Harmon's eyes expressed her concern. Perhaps she had misjudged Ivy Bly after all.

"I know this one," Mrs. Sawbuck's entire body shook with agitation.

Every man, woman, and child in the dining room turned to stare at Ivy. It was a terrible moment, maybe the worst in a succession of terrible moments over the last two days.

"I know this one and her father very well. Troublemakers, I should tell you right now, Sergeant Harmon. Nothing but a pair of troublemakers. Peas in a pod, those two. First, he gets in a fist fight with two elderly clients, and I have to break it up. Then the next thing I know the girl hides in the bathroom and the father makes a racket that could rouse the dead. I had a fit trying to quiet them down. Almost called the police over here myself." Mrs. Sawbuck paused to catch her breath. "I am not surprised the two of them are in trouble now. Bound for trouble, the both of them. That's what I told myself. The more you do to help some people, the worse it gets."

Ivy's mouth frowned with anger, and a beet color reddened her face. "It's not true," she whispered to the sergeant.

"Not true?" Mrs. Sawbuck was whipped into a fury. "Ask anyone of these people here. Go on, Sergeant Harmon, ask them."

"That won't be necessary," Betty said quietly.

"No, it will be necessary." Sawbuck's hand swept around the dining room. "I won't be called a liar. Now, didn't you see this girl's father beat up two old men and raise the worst fuss ever heard in the halls of the *BUENA VISTA CENTER FOR THE UNFORTUNATE?*"

Where before all eyes had been turned to Ivy, now each one of those eyes returned to the business of eating.

"Well?" Mrs. Sawbuck sounded exactly like the squealing brakes on Betty Harmon's police car. "Is anyone going to answer?"

Finally, from across the room one small voice offered, "That fight weren't none of his fault. That fight belonged to two bums who were so drunk they could have stabbed each other and not even knowed about it."

"Yeah," a couple of others joined in.

"So," Mrs. Sawbuck's skinny face inflated with disgust, "you can't expect one speck of loyalty from these people. They are impossible," and she turned on her heels and stormed into the hall. She returned briskly to her office, while Sergeant Harmon and Ivy trailed behind.

"She doesn't like us," Ivy said.

"I can tell."

As soon as the three had reseated themselves, Mrs. Sawbuck commenced her reproval, "Tell us why you ran away, Ivy?"

The girl winced at the sound of her name.

"After Sergeant Harmon was kind enough to bring you here to find your friend, you repay her by taking off. Do you think that's right? Or do you go around doing whatever pleases you?"

Ivy was silent, afraid to answer, afraid that whatever she said would be misinterpreted and distorted. The two women's four eyes penetrated her own. Obviously, Sergeant Harmon was waiting for Ivy to explain her behavior.

"I don't know," Ivy said with desperation. "I don't know, I don't know."

"Were you trying to run away, Ivy?" Betty's voice was both kind and stern.

"I don't know," Ivy repeated. "I'm not sure. I don't know."

Mrs. Sawbuck interrupted, "It's clear that she is a confused girl. I've known that since the first day I saw her and her father. They're quite a duo. He walks around with airs, you know what I mean? Like a prince without a penny to his name. A few days ago the two of them came in here, dragging their wet belongings down the hall. Made a mess of everything. Not a dry inch of clothing on them, and the girl here with a cut on her head that warranted medical attention. I tried to say something to them then, but the father is stuck-up and cannot be bothered with my advice. He shooed me away and told me to mind my own business. Watching after homeless people is my business, and it's not my fault if some of them can't take help. It's a combination of pride and stupidity, if you ask me."

"Poppy is not stupid," Ivy protested.

"There, there," Betty soothed. "She's not talking about your father." Then turning to Mrs. Sawbuck, "Do you know anything about this Clarisse?"

"I know who she is. She's another one who is stuck-up. Always walking around as if she bought her clothes in a French boutique, but she gets them the same as everyone else around here — out of a donation box."

"Would you have any idea where this Clarisse usually stays?"

"Stays?" Mrs. Sawbuck snorted. "She probably stays on the street because she's usually here in the morning taking an hour in the bathroom. We've had plenty of complaints about her, too."

Betty shook her head. It was obvious that Sawbuck was going to be of little help.

"You could always leave the girl here," the woman glared from behind the desk. "We'll find an extra cot for her."

Ivy froze. It was generally men, some drugged or drunk, who spent their nights at the *BUENA VISTA CENTER FOR THE UNFORTUNATE*. Poppy would die if he knew that Ivy faced the possibility of passing a night there without him. The girl made an impulsive motion towards the door, figuring her chances on the street were safer than in the shelter.

"Well, thank you," the sergeant sighed, grabbing Ivy's hand before anything rash occurred. "We'll be going now."

"There's another thing you might want to know about these two," Mrs. Sawbuck whined.

"Yes?" Sergeant Harmon asked, holding tightly onto Ivy.

"They've been getting quite a few telephone calls here all evening."

Betty turned with surprise. "From whom?"

"From a man who sounds like he's on his death bed. I can bare-ly understand him. His voice is as quiet as a spider's. You know the kind? When people talk softly like that, I get suspicious. Don't you?"

"It's Mr. Orr, Sergeant Harmon," Ivy cried out with excite-ment. "It's the people who live at *Tosca*."

"Did this man say anything?" Betty pursued.

"He identified himself as Oscar somebody, but I couldn't catch the last name. I asked him if he was a relative, but he said he was a friend. He also mumbled something about his dog going out on a walk with the girl, and the father going out to look for them. The dog came home alone a few hours ago, and he asked me if I knew what happened to the two of them. He said he and his sister were worried."

"That's Eugenia Orr, the opera singer I told you about," Ivy clasped her hands together. "She sings every time she opens her mouth."

"When he calls back," Mrs. Sawbuck continued, "I guess that I can tell him they're in jail."

Sergeant Harmon took a card with her name and number from the pocket by her badge. "This is for Clarisse. If you see her, you can ask her to get in touch with me."

"Sure, sure," Mrs. Sawbuck said.

"And this Oscar, did he leave any message?"

"The last time he called, he left this." Mrs. Sawbuck pulled a piece of note paper from a pad with a number scribbled across it and handed it over to Sergeant Harmon.

Chapter 21

FROM THE POLICE CAR BETTY HARMON DIALED THE SEVEN DIGIT number. She hoped, as Ivy hoped, that Oscar Orr or his sister would answer the ring. However, after several attempts, the sergeant gave up.

"I guess no answer won't help us," she said, consoling Ivy.

Ivy said nothing. Instead, she sat in stone silence, fidgeting with the obsidian rocks in her pocket, pondering why everything was so wrong.

They recrossed the wide, wet lanes of Market Street and entered the city's financial district. Sheaves of glass and steel skyscrapers towered over the car like inscrutable giants. Lights flickered from their highest stories, but there was no one on the dark streets.

"Are you hungry?" The sergeant asked.

Ivy honestly didn't know. Instead of yearnings for donuts and ice cream, her stomach was stuffed with worry. Poppy was detained at the police station, and her own future was filled with apprehensions and unknowns.

"I think we'd better eat. Then you'll feel better."

Betty parked in the center of North Beach, the old Italian section of San Francisco, where the streets were bustling with pedestrian traffic. Small cafes and restaurants lined the sidewalk. Neon lights flashed colorful signs across the night. Smells of olive oil, garlic, and tomato sauce mingled in the air. Swarms of people ambled festively around despite the storm.

Ivy followed Sergeant Harmon to the red striped awning which shaded the entrance to PREGO. *Authentic Home-Style Milanese Cooking* was scrawled underneath the name.

On a dozen small tables draped in red-and-white checkered cloths was placed a single red candle, a vase with one red carnation, and settings of silverware wrapped in white damask napkins. There were no customers at any of the tables, and a short, stout dark-haired woman stood behind the bar.

"Sergeant Harmon, welcome!" The buxom woman shouted out in a voice robust with accents, pronouncing more than the usual number of syllables in those three words.

"Signora Quartuccio," Betty replied warmly. "Dinner for two."

The signora's dark curls swished and swirled, and her gold hoop earrings jangled vivaciously.

"This is my young friend, Ivy Bly," Betty made the introductions.

"Signorina Bly," the signora took Ivy's hand into her plump palm. "You like Italian food, no?"

Ivy shook her head "yes."

"Then I give for you my special sauce, Sergeant Harmon's favorite dish, no?"

"Thank you, yes," Ivy said.

"*Buono*," Signora Quartuccio smiled, and the gold filling in her front tooth reflected the candlelight on the table. "Zuppa first, no?"

"Yes," Betty agreed, "we'll start with minestrone soup."

As the bowl was placed before her, Ivy shuddered over the aromatic liquid. Her face crumpled in pain as she imagined her father alone in the police station. "Excuse me," the girl suddenly rose, leaving her soup to cool and the sergeant to wonder.

On the way to the ladies' room, she passed Signora Quartuccio with a tray of homemade sourdough buns and tall glasses of water.

"Poppy!" Ivy cried to the mirror over the sink. Her own eyes spoke an accusation. Wasn't it her fault? Tears of despair were the answer.

"Signorina," a cheerful voice outside the restroom door said, "your dinner is calling."

Ivy splashed her face, doused her hair, washed her neck, and returned to her meal with little hope.

"Everything is going to be all right," Betty said with assurance. "But you must eat."

Now Ivy needed no invitation to dive into the delicious vegetable minestrone soup. She was ravenous.

"Poppy took me to a French restaurant on my tenth birthday," she related proudly.

"Oh?" Betty looked with pleasure at Ivy gobbling spoonfuls of soup.

"We were celebrating because he had just sold two paintings. He told me I could have anything on the menu, and I ordered three desserts."

"You can have anything you want here too, but Signora Quartuccio's special spaghetti sauce from Milan is famous."

"Famous?" Ivy glanced around the room of empty tables, disbelieving that the place had any reputation at all.

As if reading her thoughts, Betty responded, "People like to come here late to eat. It will be packed by ten o'clock."

There was a long pause filled with the sounds of eating. Then Betty resumed the conversation, hoping to discover a bit more information about this girl and her family. "So your father is an artist, Ivy?"

"Yes," the girl said quietly, "a very good painter, I heard."

"What do you mean?"

"The critics said he was good, and once he showed his work at a gallery in Los Angeles."

"That's impressive, but what do you think of his paintings?"

"I don't understand them," Ivy sighed, "but I guess no one else does either. He hasn't sold a painting in over two years."

"It is a difficult way to make a living and support a family."

"I guess so," Ivy sighed loudly again.

Ivy gratefully ate every morsel of Signora Quartuccio's spaghetti with the special sauce from Milan, and afterwards asked Sergeant Harmon if she might have another bowl of soup.

"I am honored," the signora replied, "but I only bring you one little cup. I want you to save yourself for my desserts. You like desserts, no?"

Ivy waved her head "yes."

"I bet you like ice cream too, no?"

"I love ice cream," Ivy exclaimed.

"*Buono*, for I got in my kitchen back there a big treat for you."

Ivy now started to feel full. She leaned back in her chair to luxuriate in the feeling. The candlelight flickered across the checkered tablecloth, and Sergeant Harmon smiled at Ivy with satisfaction.

However, the moment of contentment was brief. "What's going to happen to me?" Ivy asked plaintively. "What's going to happen after we finish dinner?"

"I'm not sure," Betty hesitated. "The first thing to do is find out how your father is."

"Maybe they have let him go by now." Ivy's hand clasped in prayer. "It wasn't his fault, not any of it. It was mine."

"He's been a good father to you?" Sergeant Harmon repeated her earlier tact, still looking for clues that might betray any lack of love between father and daughter.

"They think he's a criminal, don't they? They think he's a vagrant." Ivy pronounced the last word in a shamed, hushed voice.

"Vagrant is a person without a settled home. In fact, that does describe your situation, but there are many of you now. It's not a crime for your father to have lost his job or been unable to sell his paintings. It's not a crime to have been evicted from your house.

However, it is against the law to walk on highways where you're not allowed to go."

Ivy shrugged. She knew they weren't holding Poppy for illegally tramping along a highway. "What if they don't let my father go?"

"I've already told you. It will then be necessary to find a place for you to sleep until it's clear what the further proceedings are."

Ivy slouched in her chair. Every feature on her face drooped in a frown.

"I've decided you can stay at my place," Sergeant Harmon offered. "Would you like that?"

"I'd like that a lot," Ivy exhaled with relief. At least, one immediate problem was settled. If Poppy was still in jail, she would sleep at Sergeant Harmon's.

Through the swinging doors Signora Quartuccio reappeared from the kitchen. "I think I join you for dessert, no?" She carried a tray with three bowls of ice cream, two slices of chocolate cake, and a plate of biscotti.

"Please," Sergeant Harmon motioned to the chair between her and Ivy.

"But before we eat, I put on some music. What is life without music? That is the question I ask my American friends. And they agree with me. They agree that life is nothing, nothing, *niente* without music."

Despite her surplus weight, Signora Quartuccio moved gracefully, appearing to glide to the far side of the bar where several clicks of a tape machine were followed by a beautiful song.

"You like Italian ice cream, no?" The signora asked.

"I've never eaten ice cream like this before." Ivy looked down at the gigantic brick of pink, white, and brown confection.

"Neapolitan means it originated in Naples, a city at the southern tip of the boot. Me? I serve authentic Milanese cooking from the north, coming from Milan, but I cannot resist the ice cream, *gelato* Italians say, from the south. Vanilla, strawberry, and chocolate. That is the way we Italians are. We say instead of choosing a favorite, why not put them all together? It's good, no?"

Ivy took a bite of the ice cream. "It's delicious."

"Now for an Italian cookie, no?"

"Yes," Ivy said emphatically, beginning to tire of Signora Quartuccio asking "no" whenever she meant "yes."

"Yes, yes," the signora handed over the plate of biscotti. The dry, narrow biscuits were the color of adobe, smooth on two sides, riddled with slivers of almond, and hard as cement.

"Dip it in the ice cream to soften it," Signora Quartuccio suggested, scooping a bit of ice cream from her plate with the dry cookie. "Like this, no?"

Ivy and Sergeant Harmon followed suit, shoveling ice cream with biscotti and listening to the swelling sounds of the music.

"Soon the people will start to arrive," Signora Quartuccio said with great pride. "Soon all the tables will be filled, and the cooks will be complaining."

Except for the threesome, the restaurant was still empty.

"Soon it will begin. With the clattering and the chattering, we will not hear one note of opera. Every night I sit and watch the door for the first customer. Once in a while someone comes early like you, but usually they wait. They wait, and I wait too. Sometimes I think, tonight they won't come. But I am always wrong. Always they come in droves to eat my special sauce from Milano. Then there are too many of them. They have to wait in line for tables. They wait late in the night. They wait in the rain. The cooks run out of pasta, and it is so noisy, I cannot hear one note of my opera. They eat and drink their red wine. They pay, and they go home. Afterwards it is empty and quiet again, and the music sings to me."

The signora's arms danced in the air, her bright eyes blinking, her gold tooth flashing above her red painted lips. Suddenly, she motioned for silence and folded her hands in reverence. For a moment, she didn't stir. Then quietly, with dignity and calm, the signora began to weep large tears. Watching her made Ivy and Sergeant Harmon weep, too. It was the sweet strains of pain in the music. Someone was singing with pure beauty, and the sweetness of that beauty derived from something very sad. Ivy listened and thought about her own sadness.

When the song ended, Signora Quartuccio removed a handkerchief from her waistband and wiped the rims of her eyes. "For me there is nothing that compares to *Tosca's* aria except great love, and that is more rare than a tape recording, no?" Signora Quartuccio smiled through her tears, brushing the top of Ivy's rough hand. "It is beautiful, yes?"

"*Tosca*," Ivy could barely contain herself, "Signora Quartuccio said *Tosca*. That is the name of the house where my Poppy and I were. Remember the picture I drew?"

"Of course, I remember. It was a lovely drawing."

"*Tosca*, my child, you know *Tosca?*" Signora Quartuccio grasped Ivy's wrist. "This American child knows *Tosca?* Ah, it is my favorite opera. It is Puccini, and in this song, *Tosca* is singing with a wretched heart because her lover is being tortured by *Scarpia* in the next room. She can hear his cries of torture through the walls. Oh, *Scarpia*, he is an evil man, and *Tosca* is a beautiful woman. So it is very sad," she repeated in Italian, "*molto triste*, very sad."

"Ivy knows many things for a child her age," Sergeant Harmon added.

"Yes," the signora nodded, touching Ivy's fingertips. "Perhaps like *Tosca*, she has suffered, too."

Chapter 22

"WE MUST BE GOING," SERGEANT HARMON SAID.

"No?" The signora exclaimed with disbelief. "Going so soon?"

Betty nodded.

"But, but," the signora stammered. "Before the customers arrive, before the cooks start complaining, let us listen together. Now it is good. Now it is quiet."

Sergeant Harmon pulled several bills from her wallet and checked her watch. "We probably should go."

"One little aria, Sergeant Harmon. One tiny little Puccini aria to send you out into this stormy night." Turning to Ivy, the signora asked, "You remember what I say, no?"

Ivy's mind fumbled. During the course of their dinner, the signora had said so many strange things.

"Of course, you remember," Signora Quartuccio continued. "Life is nothing without music. So tonight I am certain Sergeant Harmon will let us enjoy this *magnifico* musical moment. Yes? No?"

"Of course," Betty Harmon agreed. "After all, it will only take a few minutes."

The signora rewound a portion of the tape while Sergeant Harmon and Ivy sat waiting for the music to begin, but just as Signora Quartuccio touched the button to start, she paused again. "Ivy, I want to tell you about this *bellissima* soprano, yes?"

"Signora," Sergeant Harmon let out a gentle sigh. "I don't want to be rude."

"Then don't be," the signora snapped. "It will take one second to explain."

"I told police headquarters that we'd be back by now."

Ignoring the sergeant's concerns, Signora Quartuccio continued, "There are many artists whom you hear in this recording." As the signora spoke, she made grander and grander, higher and higher gestures with her arms, while her eyes glistened like jet beads. "There is, of course, Puccini, the composer. There are the musicians who play his music. But the artist who sings, Signorina Ivy, this is a gift placed into the throats of few."

"Who is it? Who is singing?" Ivy asked excitedly.

"In my very small opinion, it is the greatest *Tosca* who ever lived. I heard 'La Magnifica' sing when I was only a girl Signorina Bly's age. My mother took me to La Scala in Milano to hear her. The entire audience wept. Seats and floors were flooded with our tears." Signora Quartuccio pushed the button of the tape, and her voice announced loudly, sharply, clearly, "Listen to the great soprano, Eugenia Orr, sing *Tosca*. Listen to her pouring out her heart."

"Who?" Ivy and Sergeant Harmon jumped from their seats and

shouted in unison.

"Shusssh," the signora made a threatening gesture. "The great Eugenia Orr."

The singer's sonorous voice flooded the spaces of the room. Ivy, Betty Harmon, and the signora sat motionless with the beauty and pain in the music and the voice. Signora Quartuccio had to use her handkerchief to wipe away the tears, but for Ivy there was no sadness. This time she listened to Miss Orr sing as if they were in conversation, as if she could now call on the telephone and ask her to send Oscar over to pick them up. The distance between them vanished. Miss Orr was here. Ivy was here. The girl felt the special rocks in her pocket. Maybe her mother was here, too. Soon everything would be right again. Together, they would get Poppy away from the horrid jail.

"What is it you wanted to say, Signorina Bly? When the music was starting, I couldn't hear you. I couldn't think. I could only listen. But now, I am with you again. Speak, speak to me."

"Miss Orr, Miss Orr, she is our friend! It was her house we were trying to find. Oh, signora! Oh, sergeant!"

Sergeant Harmon tried to explain, "It is possible that Ivy knows this Eugenia Orr."

"Have you met the great diva?" The signora looked at Ivy with pride. "How fortunate you are, my girl, for you have met the voice of the century. I think you must be an extraordinary young lady yourself. Extraordinary, no?"

Ivy beamed. She had spent the last several months feeling less than extraordinary. Although Poppy tried to tell her there were special things about her, it had recently become hard to believe. After all, a father was supposed to find good things in a daughter, but now Sergeant Harmon and Signora Quartuccio had said it, too. "Extraordinary" was a delicious word, and it rolled around Ivy's brain like a rare marble.

"Do you too happen to know Eugenia Orr?" Sergeant Harmon delicately asked the signora. "I have heard that she lives in San Francisco," she added, winking at Ivy.

"I know her only a precious little bit," the signora boasted. "She is very old now. No one knows how old, but I would venture to guess the great diva is past eighty, maybe ninety."

"She is very old," Ivy piped in.

Signora Quartuccio continued, "Her brother is quite old, too."

"Oscar, dear Oscar," Ivy interrupted. "He has already helped us so much."

"Occasionally, Miss Eugenia and the brother dine here. Miss Eugenia says the cooking reminds her of the times she spent at La Scala in Milano. You know I make the authentic Milanese cooking, no? Many like it, but there are only a few who truly appreciate it. Miss Eugenia Orr and the brother are among them." In that instant Signora Quartuccio's pride was unbounded.

"Would you have their telephone number, by chance?"

"Oh no, no, no, no, no, no, no, no! They are very private, very famous people, yes? They do not give out their telephone number. They rarely go out. They are both very old."

"I know, I know!" Ivy cried. "That's why they want Poppy to help them. They need someone to fix things."

"Aaaahhh," the signora sighed, "of course. They need help. They are so old now."

"We have a number, but no one answers. I think it is the wrong number, but if you could possibly get their number for us, I would appreciate it," Sergeant Harmon said.

The signora puzzled over the request, admitting gravely, "I do not know anyone who has either their address or their telephone number."

Ivy's head lowered with disillusion. While *Tosca* had been playing, contact with the Orr's had seemed so real. Now, it was only a remote and far-fetched possibility again.

Sergeant Harmon and Ivy put on their jackets to go.

"You Americans have an expression for it, yes?" The signora complained. "You say you don't like to eat and run, but look at you. Life is too short to be eating and running. Next time you must promise to stay longer, yes? And eat more, no?"

With her hands on Ivy's shoulders, Sergeant Harmon guided them to the front entrance for a final farewell. As Ivy touched its handle, the door turned from the outside and a small dog ran through the entry and jumped straight into the girl's arms. Behind him appeared the large figure of Oscar Orr, who at the sight of Ivy, threw his unlit cigar onto the floor and embraced her.

"My child, ye have worried the sister and me sick with ye and ye father's absence. We were pacing and worrying, and Dice was running under the kitchen table like to have a fit since he couldn't talk to us outright. We didn't know what to think all evening, and tonight sister said to me that the only thing that might calm her was the taste of Signora Quartuccio's spaghetti sauce from Milan."

"Dice!" Ivy murmured as the dog whimpered lovingly in reply, wriggling between the girl's arms, burrowing his head in her armpit, licking her neck and chin with slobbering affection.

"I guess those two know each other," Sergeant Harmon said.

"They certainly do," Oscar confirmed. "The wee dog has been in deep lamentation ever since he reappeared solo early this evening. The sister, Eugenia, told me to go out and find the humans so I took the Cadillac and looked all over town. I ventured down to the *BUENA VISTA CENTER FOR THE UNFORTU-NATE*, I did, but ye can't get cooperation from those people. They said they didn't know ye and never heard of ye." Oscar was breathless. "Yes, it has been one sad sight at *Tosca* tonight. Dice crying, sister sighing. I called the police, but ye see, we didn't know the Poppy's last name, and nobody there seemed capable of figuring out if a man and a big wee girl had stopped by or not."

Signora Quartuccio clutched Oscar's arm, "Signor Orr, brother of the great diva, it is a privilege to have you in my restaurant this evening, yes? We were just listening to *Tosca* in a recording by your sister, no? And I said to the signorina that she was the greatest singer of the century, yes? As always we are pleased and honored to see you, no?"

Befuddled with the "yes" and "no" questions at the end of each sentence, Oscar stood shaking his head, confused as to what he should answer.

"Mr. Orr?" Sergeant Harmon poised with her pencil above her notepad.

"Yes, that I am."

"You know Ivy Bly, I presume?"

"Not so well, but well enough. The sister and I, we were hoping to have her and the Poppy stay at the house for a while and help us with odds and ends. Ye see, we are getting along in years and can't do everything around such a big place."

"They were picked up by a patrol car walking on the highway. I believe there was dog with them, too," Sergeant Harmon explained.

"Yes! This is the dog Dice," Ivy cried out, stroking the creature's checkered coat.

"Sergeant, I shall tell ye how it is." Oscar's voice rose for the occasion. "The sister and I, we came home from the doctor's to the house and found the kitchen cleaned like new. That was a thrill, for the doctor ordered us to find someone to help, and we were hoping these two might climb aboard. Such a big house could use a couple more warm bodies. So we sat down for a nice cup of tea to discuss the matter with the Poppy, and he told us that the girl and dog left on a walk, but the weather was, ye see, turning very bad, and naturally he was anxious and concerned. Time passed, and the girl Ivy here, and the dog Dice there, did not return, so a very agitated Poppy set out to fetch them. The hours went by until it was pure dark outside, and the dog came trotting up the backstairs whimpering like he was lost. It wasn't he who was lost, but those two." Oscar turned and pointed his finger at Ivy. "Looks like I found one of them right here."

"That is a wonderful story, Signor Orr." Signora Quartuccio clapped her hands with delight.

"Signora," Oscar said most seriously, "that is neither a story nor a tale. That is the truth. The sister and I have been worried to death, and at our advanced age, that is a serious and threatening condition."

"Yes, yes, yes," the signora prattled on. "What can I fix this evening for the divine diva?"

"Nothing fancy, signora. Miss Eugenia wants a simple plate of spaghetti with the special sauce from Milan. Milanese, ye calls it. That will make her happy. And for me the same, plus a half-dozen baked garlic bulbs, a platter of clams, fried buffalo mozzarella cheese, grilled zucchini, any bones ye might have for the wee dog here, and four slices of Gateau St. Honore cake."

"Coming up right away," and waving her hands in the air, the signora flew off to the kitchen.

Chapter 23

T HE INSTANT THE POWDER-BLUE CAR TURNED INTO THE driveway, the heavy front door swung open. Every window in the large old house called *Tosca* was aflame with light, and Miss Orr stood silhouetted by the blazing crystal chandelier in the hall. There were the outlines of her long dress, her thin arms, her fingers full of rings, and her embroidered slippers. She poised as still as a statue, and the only moving part was one hand frantically waving at the Cadillac.

Dice jumped out of the car, running at Miss Eugenia, almost knocking over her wobbling body. Ivy and Poppy followed Oscar to the old woman's side where much commotion was made over the events of the evening.

"It was such good luck that we met ye both," Miss Orr sighed.

"Good luck, bad luck, ye never know," Oscar commented as usual.

"It was certainly bad luck when Ivy slipped down the ravine," Poppy reminded them, "and couldn't get back up."

"But good luck when Dice found my special obsidian rocks," Ivy offered.

"And bad luck when we got stopped by the police," Poppy followed.

"But good luck that Sergeant Harmon was so kind," Ivy reminded him.

"Followed by bad luck when Mrs. Sawbuck at the *BUENA VISTA CENTER FOR THE UNFORTUNATE* gave you the wrong telephone number."

"But good luck when we went to eat Italian food." Ivy rubbed her stomach fondly with the delicious memories of Signora Quartuccio's minestrone soup and special sauce from Milan.

"Bad luck, good luck, ye never know," Oscar repeated. "It was certainly good luck the night we found dog here in a garbage can in Paris."

"Garbage can?" Ivy giggled.

"Several years back the sister and I were strolling to our hotel on the river Seine. It was very late and the avenues were nearly empty. By *L'Opera* we heard a little peep coming from a trash can. Isn't that right, sister?"

Miss Orr was smiling gaily. She opened her large mouth and sang, "Yes."

"The sister thought it might be a rat, but I fretted it was a baby. I decided to take a look, and behold, there was little Dice, a wee pup, who had been thrown away like a shoe. The poor thing had snuggled to the edge of the can, frightened and hungry. He's a survivor, that little wee one." Oscar's big bald head shook with silent laughter, as he expertly twirled an unlit cigar like a baton between his fingers.

"I am starving for Milanese," Eugenia reminded her brother.

"St. Honore cake for all," Oscar announced, as they trooped through the front door of the house to the kitchen.

When Eugenia rose to go to bed, the others followed. Standing at the entrance to a suite of rooms on the second floor, she said, "I hope ye find it comfortable."

"Nothing could be sweeter," Poppy sighed as he surveyed the bed with its old-fashioned feather mattress, its pile of pillows and down comforters.

"For the child," Eugenia continued, "I've made up a trundle nearby. That way she'll feel comfortable until ye become more acquainted with the place."

It had been months since Ivy and Poppy had slept in real beds with actual sheets, on pillows covered with clean pillowcases, under warm blankets and thick quilts. That night they slept like human logs.

Late the next morning, Poppy made his living arrangements with the Orr's. Although he had fallen on hard times, he said he could accept no charity.

Miss Orr said that if Poppy were willing to stick around, there was plenty of work and decent pay to do it. She offered him room and board for Ivy and himself plus a salary.

"An offer I can't refuse," Poppy said proudly. He had examined the premises and figured there was enough to keep him gainfully employed for months. Besides roof tiles to fix, chimneys and gutters to clear, yard maintenance and gardening to do, cracks to fill, broken windows to replace, every surface cried out for overall cleaning, painting, and repair. "We don't want to impose."

"Impose, Mister Poppy?"

"As soon as I've saved enough to get our own place, we'll move on."

"Mister Poppy, the brother and I weren't born into money, but my voice made me quite a bit. We have had a grand time with it, but now it's a wee bit lonely. Money bought us all this space, but no life to put into it. Ye stay as long as it's comfortable."

As Poppy predicted, there were endless chores at *Tosca*, and the weeks flew by. Meanwhile, the foul winter weather finally cleared, and the days grew warm. Buds sprang out on rose bushes and fruit trees, and bulbs, such as tulips, hyacinth, and daffodils, appeared overnight.

Poppy's days were occupied with work, Ivy's afternoons with study. Oscar puttered in the yard, and Miss Orr accompanied herself constantly in song at the baby grand piano. Dice occupied himself with the usual doggy activities of eating, running, sleeping, and barking. Ivy could not remember a time when she had ever been happier.

One evening at dinner, Poppy shyly offered a proposal of his own. "Before things started to go wrong," he said modestly, "I was a painter of paintings."

"Ah," Miss Orr's words trilled like a brook, "we can tell that by everything ye do. Ye have an artist's touch."

"Well," Poppy fumbled, almost too timid to make his request. "I am wondering if I might take it up again in a little corner of your attic."

"Ye aren't comfortable in the rooms near the landing?" Oscar asked with concern.

"The sleeping is perfectly fine, but I was hoping to paint again in my spare time. You see, I'd like to fix up a spot to work in the evenings. The attic is ideal. The dormer window faces north, and if I'm up there, no one will smell the stinky turpentine."

"Splendid!" Miss Orr proclaimed. "It's a splendid idea. *Atelier* is what we call an artist's studio in Paris, and Mister Poppy, there is no reason why ye shan't have an *atelier* here at *Tosca*."

Poppy's tired eyes shone with the excitement of his old dreams.

"Most everyone we know is dead," Oscar mused, "but we could invite in the four or five left to see ye work."

"Yes, Mister Poppy, ye paint ye paintings, and we shall have a gallery show downstairs here. We shall make a party to admire them."

"No need to make a fuss," Poppy protested. "Nobody knows who I am."

"That doesn't matter a whit." Eugenia's voice rose toward high C. "For a few still know who I am."

"Signora Quartuccio gets quite a crowd." Oscar suggested, "We can advertise ye at her restaurant."

"No, no!" Poppy cried, his hands and brow wet with anxiety. "I haven't painted in a year. Right now I don't have a single painting to show. I'm not sure if my hands will work or if the brushes will have anything to say."

"Of course, you have something to say, Poppy." Ivy climbed onto her father's lap. "Of course, you can paint. You've painted your whole life."

"Maybe that's so," Poppy nodded, "but I'm unsure of myself now. I'm shaky. I have no expectations. A little studio will be sufficient, Miss Orr, to see if there's any juice left in my blood. If I start planning shows or ringing up sales, it might bring me bad luck."

"Bad luck, good luck," Oscar whispered his proverbial refrain, "ye never know."

"True, true," Poppy laughed, and with that, good cheer spread contagiously around the table.

"Now that we've settled the business of Mister Poppy's *atelier*, shall I tell ye a story?" Oscar asked.

All approved, including Dice, who was suddenly alert and on his feet again.

"In China," Oscar began, "there was an old farmer whose prize stallion ran away. When the villagers heard the news, they walked out to the farm to console the old man on his bad luck. Like me, the farmer responded, 'Bad luck, good luck. Who knows?' The villagers nodded and returned home.

"The next day when the old farmer awoke, the prize stallion had returned from the hills, followed by twelve lovely mares. The villagers once again walked out to the farm, this time to congratulate the man on his good luck. But like me, the farmer only replied, 'Bad luck, good luck. Who knows?'

"The following day, while trying to break one of the mares, the farmer's only son was thrown to the ground. One of his legs was badly broken, and he was put to bed in great pain. The villagers heard of the accident and walked out to the farm to commiserate. The old man merely said, 'Bad luck, good luck. Who knows?'

"The very next day, the Chinese army swept through the area and took away every able-bodied man under thirty for a soldier, leaving the village in mourning. Because of his injury, the farmer's son was the only young man spared. In the evening the villagers walked out to the old man's place to celebrate his good luck, but the farmer had only one thing to say, like me — 'Bad luck, good luck. Who knows?'"

"Doesn't it go on?" Ivy pleaded, for it was the kind of story she wished would never end.

"It goes on forever," Oscar chuckled, "but that's all I know."

"Mister Poppy, no one will mention ye paintings, just in case it's bad luck," Miss Orr promised. "But ye are welcome to have a place to paint."

Chapter 24

IVY COLLAPSED ON THE WINDOW SEAT, ABSENTLY TOSSING HER three obsidian rocks. Up and down like jacks, they went from air to palm, sparkling as if they were immersed in water.

"So tell me, child, about the rocks that ye and Dice risked life and limb to find?" Eugenia Orr asked from her bench at the piano.

"There's not much to tell, Miss Orr. I would much rather hear something about you."

"Then we'll make a barter. Ye tell me about the rocks, and I'll tell ye about the rings."

Ivy stared at Miss Orr's wrinkled fingers. Indeed, she would like to know about her beautiful jewels — the deep, quiet emerald; the red throbbing ruby; the sapphire whose color reflected Miss Eugenia's grey-blue-violet eyes; the diamond as clear as water; and the pearl that bubbled like champagne.

"Would ye like to try them on? That is, if I can get any of them off my crooked fingers."

The emerald and ruby bands were too small for Ivy, the sapphire and diamond could barely slip across the knuckle of her smallest finger, but the pearl, her favorite, shimmied onto Ivy's index finger and glimmered like a full moon.

"From the looks of it, I don't think these are any more precious than ye rocks there. Am I right?"

Ivy loved the sound of the old woman's voice traveling over the syllables of words like musical notes.

"Poppy thinks I'm a little bit crazy," the girl said softly, holding the black objects next to the shimmering pearl.

"If ye hadn't already noticed, I am not your Poppy," Eugenia grimaced a keen imitation of Poppy's most unpleasant expression, "but I can look like him if I try very hard."

Ivy grinned at Miss Orr's mimicry.

"It is highly doubtful that I shall find ye crazy or foolish, child."

"They are plain rocks, after all," Ivy paused, embarrassed as to how to explain the significance of her most valued and most private possession.

"I think not," Miss Orr shook her head and a thick strand of hair loosened from her bun.

"I found them in the place where we buried my mother," the girl blurted more loudly than she had intended.

"And where might that be?"

"A few hundred miles north and east of here on Mount Shasta."

"A beautiful spot, no doubt, although I have never been there." Miss Orr spoke as if she were singing instead of prying.

Ivy lifted her drawing pad from the window sill and quickly sketched a picture of a large conical mountain capped with snow. "There," she said, adding wildflowers and billows of clouds to the borders of the mountainside.

"It is a volcano then." Miss Orr's eyes peered at the drawing, studying each of its details. "Maybe you and Mister Poppy can take me to Mount Shasta some day."

"It is the most beautiful spot on earth."

"And ye mother's bones are there?"

"No, her ashes, and I took these rocks when I was little, thinking they were part of her." Ivy said shyly, ashamed now of her childishness.

"Not crazy at all, child. Surely, they are. Surely, you have made it so."

Miss Orr studied the rocks while Ivy fingered the large, mysterious pearl. When Miss Orr spoke again, her voice was uncharacteristically awkward and small. "When I was a wee girl, my parents took me on the train from my home in Glasgow, Scotland to London for a visit to an aunt. Soon after we arrived at Victoria Station, someone kidnaped me."

"How terrible!" Ivy gasped.

"Yes, a man kidnaped me out of the station." Miss Orr smiled quietly. "Maybe it was terrible, but I don't remember a thing. In fact, my mother told me that the whole night I was gone, she prayed that if I were ever found alive, I would remember nothing."

Ivy gaped in horror.

"Don't ye know that her prayer came true? The next morning a policeman found me in a street in Chelsea, and I never recalled one thing that happened."

"But why did your mother make that prayer? I want to remember everything," Ivy said urgently.

Miss Orr searched to explain, "You see, my mother thought if something horrible had befallen me, it might ruin my life. It might fill me with fear and terror for the rest of my days. With such a painful memory, my childhood would be ended. She thought I might never sing or play again. So she prayed that I forget."

"I am afraid to forget," Ivy confessed, "afraid that if I don't remember my mother, she'll disappear. She'll dissolve into nothing. At least, these rocks are evidence of her existence."

"I tell ye this story because bad things happen to many children. Losing ye mother and father is the worst that can happen, but ye still have one around who loves ye, Ivy. Am I right?" Miss Orr clasped her hands gleefully, "One day I shall insist that Mister Poppy drive us to this Mount Shasta."

Ivy handed Miss Orr the obsidian rocks.

"Ah, they are very heavy and very black, but they are lovely," Eugenia sighed. "They must give ye comfort now and then to have them."

"They do. Sometimes I talk to them and hug them. Sometimes I pretend that they are my mother. I pretend that she's not dead."

"I'm sure ye mother must have been lovely."

"I think so." One lonely tear deserted Ivy's eye for her cheek. She didn't want to cry, but she couldn't help it. It was never easy talking to anyone about her mother.

"I'll go make us tea, child," Miss Orr said kindly, "and when I return, I'll tell ye about my rings."

Eugenia's delicate old hands carried a lacquer tray, two Wedgewood saucers and cups, a silver sugar bowl, a pitcher of cream, and a round, generous teapot of Earl Grey.

"My mother told me another thing, child," Miss Orr settled on the window seat beside Ivy. "She lived to be over ninety and had a good life, bless her soul. Whenever I had a bad thing on my mind, a sad thing I couldn't shake loose, not a small or a trivial thing, mind ye, but something large and hopeless, maybe a secret that no one else could know, maybe a place I hurt deep inside, she said that I should go and tell the dreadful thing to a tree. She told me to hug a tree and give it my secret. Let the tree help take care of it for me, my mother said. That way I wouldn't have to carry it around by myself." Miss Orr's chuckle sounded like rain. "Silly, hey? Some might think it silly or crazy or foolish, but every tree out there has at least one of my secrets."

Ivy leaned out the window to view the dozen trees in *Tosca's* front yard. Sycamore, horse chestnut, eucalyptus, mimosa, palm, and magnolia cast stately late afternoon shadows across the newly mowed lawn.

"So many?" Ivy asked cautiously.

"Oh yes, when ye have lived as long as I have, there are many secrets and many sadnesses."

"And what about Oscar? Does he tell his secrets to trees?"

"Indeed. Sometimes I see him hugging the magnolia over there and crying a wee bit. You see, almost everyone we love is gone now. His wife and children, my husbands too."

"You were married?" Ivy could not imagine Miss Orr as a bride.

"Yes, child. I had two husbands, but I outlived them both. My first one passed away when he was only twenty-five. He died of yellow fever in Barcelona in 1926." Miss Orr gathered a stack of musty picture albums from the shelf above the piano, brushing the layers of dust away with her skirt. "I haven't looked at these things in years. It's best not to be too sentimental, but here he is." Eugenia held up a page with a dim photo of a short dark man. "He was the most handsome man and the greatest bullfighter in all of Spain. How I loved him." Miss Orr's voice rang out like a line of operatic verse. "He gave me this on our first anniversary." The sapphire ring flashed like a beacon.

"Is that you?" Ivy asked. To the left of the man was a view of a mountain lake and to the right was a tall, gay woman in a wide-brim hat.

"Yes, we were on our honeymoon in the French Alps."

"What about the diamond ring?"

"Ah, the diamond came from my mother's mother. The ruby was a gift from an admirer of my singing, a South American tycoon. The emerald arrived in my dressing room without a card."

"Without a card?" Ivy asked in dismay.

"I never learned who sent it."

"And the pearl?" Ivy was eager to know the story of her favorite.

"My dearly departed second husband found that pearl himself diving off an island in the South Pacific. That was between the two Great Wars."

"The Great Wars?" Ivy puzzled.

"The First and Second World Wars," Eugenia explained. "The First was a terrible, slow war. I lost my brother and two cousins in the trenches. Oscar lost his son in the Second." Pointing to the huge palm tree at the far end of the drive, she added, "It is comforting to tell the grand one over there all about it."

Ivy leaned her head on the window pane. Many times she had spoken her troubles to her rocks. The secrets of her twelve years were locked inside the hard obsidian.

At that moment Oscar, Dice, and Poppy tromped into the room. Oscar raised one of his eyebrows and twirled an unlit cigar. His eyebrow had more hair than his entire head. "Is it tea time, sister?"

"Indeed brother, and a very nice tea it is. We're here talking about old times."

More cups and crackers were fetched from the kitchen and

Dice was rewarded with a biscuit.

"Mister Poppy, Ivy has been telling me such lovely things about Mount Shasta."

"It's the most beautiful spot on earth," Poppy sighed.

"I've drawn it for her, Poppy." Ivy held up the cone-shaped mountain.

"It's more than a place," Poppy explained. "It's an entire atmosphere."

"Like Paris?" Oscar suggested.

"Like I imagine Paris," Poppy said. "I've never been to Paris, but I imagine it has a feeling, an indescribable atmosphere."

"Yes," Miss Orr enthused, "Paris is always itself."

"Exactly. Mount Shasta is always itself, too."

"Perhaps ye will take us to this Mount Shasta after your painting show?" Miss Orr insisted.

"It's possible." Poppy tried to control his urge to go to Mount Shasta that very instant.

"Ye have worked hard for many months, Mister Poppy, and when the show is finished, I propose a little vacation."

Dice barked, for the word "vacation" always sounded good to him.

"After the show you'll want to rest," Ivy said emphatically, for she had noticed how nervous the business of painting made her father.

For the past several days Poppy had rambled around in a feverish sweat, muttering his doubts as to whether the paintings were any good. Finally, he had concluded they were terrible and tried to convince Miss Orr to cancel the show, but she told him it was too late. There was no reason to let art go unobserved. In addition, she said, he was behaving like a child.

The gallery show she promised was now scheduled for the following weekend. With the help of Signora Quartuccio, Eugenia had arranged everything. Notice of the showing had been posted in the restaurant, invitations mailed to notable art patrons, word sent to critics at various newspapers, additional invites hand-delivered to Clarisse, c/o *BUENA VISTA CENTER FOR THE UNFORTUNATE* and Sergeant Betty Harmon, c/o San Francisco

Police Department. Of course, the catering would be authentic Milanese with the signora's northern Italian specialties. Everything was prepared, but Poppy was still unsure.

Tea calmed Poppy for the moment, and the mention of a get-away to Mount Shasta filled his lungs with fresh mountain air and cleared his anxious brain.

"Where does one stay at Mount Shasta?" Miss Orr asked.

"There are hotels, motels, caravansaries, inns," Poppy enumerated, "but Ivy and I camp." Then he quickly added, "I can find us a comfortable hotel without any trouble."

"Mister Poppy, that won't be necessary. We shall sleep alfresco under the stars."

"Speak for yeself, sister," Oscar grumbled. "I am not mixing with ground animals."

"Accommodations are not a problem. My concern is whether the Cadillac can make the drive."

"Precisely, Mister Poppy," Miss Orr agreed, for she had tried to persuade her brother to buy a more practical car for fifteen years. "Ye can't rely on an ancient thing."

"Ye rely plenty on me." Oscar's eyes twinkled. "I'm far more ancient than that automobile."

"Yes, and ye are getting too old to be relied on. That's why we have Mister Poppy here," Miss Orr reminded her brother.

"Ye are too much of a know-it-all," Oscar retorted indignantly. "Ye don't know the first wee thing about a car. Ye are entirely ignorant, but ye will sit here in front of Mister Poppy and tell him that the Cadillac is unfit for travel and object to my mechanical abilities."

"Mechanical abilities?" Eugenia roared like a hurricane.

The living room heated up with Orr insults and accusations. Not to be left out of the activities, Dice howled.

"Excuse me," Poppy intervened, shouting to get their attention and sending Dice to the kitchen with the point of a finger. "I believe we were discussing a journey."

"Of course, Mister Poppy, let us try to continue without interference," Oscar said.

"Ye won't have any further interference from me." Tapping her cane, Eugenia Orr clattered out of the room, slamming the door behind her.

"She'll be fine, sister will," Oscar assured Ivy. "We have to blow off steam now and again after living around each other for almost eighty years. We get on each other's nerves, but neither of us holds a grudge."

Poppy sat back, picturing the road to Mount Shasta, the moment the great mountain swelled into view, the smell of the sun on the meadows, the light of the volcano at dusk.

"So what about the Cadillac?" Poppy asked again.

"With good luck, that car will go anywhere."

"Bad luck, good luck," Poppy smiled slyly. "Who knows?"

Chapter 25

SAMUEL BLY'S PAINTING EXHIBITION AT TOSCA WAS SCHEDULED for the last Sunday in July. Unfortunately, the day was cold and foggy, typical of summers that San Francisco is famous for — days that would signal winter in other regions of the world. But as Eugenia Orr said, "The weather simply could not be helped."

"The weather is a piece of bad luck," Oscar predictably added, "but bad luck, good luck? Who knows?"

Early that morning Signora Quartuccio arrived with two young cousins to help prepare the food. Rapidly boiling sauce and flying knives overtook the kitchen, and no one in the household, including Dice, dared enter the signora's sacred domain.

In the dining room Ivy helped Miss Orr decorate the banquet table, covering it with fresh linen, glistening silver bowls, and giant serving spoons. Champagne glasses were unboxed by the dozen, and a spray of orchids in slender crystal was positioned as the centerpiece.

In the living room the piano and sofas were pushed aside into corners, every ornament and knickknack removed from shelves and walls. The Persian carpets were meticulously vacuumed and the panes of window carefully washed.

Like a circus ringmaster stationed in the room's center, Oscar directed while Poppy hung the paintings. "Up! No down! Up again! To the left! More right! No left! It's crooked!"

The directions often contradicted each other and Poppy was almost driven mad. However, his temper held, and by noon the task was done. All the paintings were properly displayed at the correct angle and height.

Until this instant not one person had visited Poppy's *atelier*. Therefore, no one other than Poppy had glimpsed the paintings. It was something of a shock even for him to view the work hung all together. For quite a few minutes, he and Oscar stood staring mutely at the walls.

Poppy was overwhelmed by how many paintings there were and how much effort it had required to paint them.

Oscar, on the other hand, was astonished by something altogether different. It was the content of the paintings that stunned the old man into speechlessness. Several were pictures of Oscar himself, displayed with a huge bald head and a dangling cigar as thick as a silver baton. Eugenia appeared bug-like with swollen magenta lips. A distorted Dice, a battered blue Cadillac, *Tosca's* weedy lawns, its dirty kitchen with dirty windows, and the back porch filled with emergency rations of canned goods were inserted into Poppy's paintings.

Oscar Orr did not know what to think and his generally friend-ly lips rigidified into two thin blue lines.

"Do you like them?" Poppy finally asked, having had his courage raised by Oscar's silent awe.

Oscar stuttered and sputtered.

"I was afraid they might offend you," Poppy hurried to explain, "but every time I tried to paint anything else, it was you who burst into my mind."

"Oh?" Oscar was shocked.

"Yes, it's true. All my fingers could do was paint you, Miss Orr, Dice, the car, and the things around here."

"Oh," Oscar muttered again, flattered that Poppy was so eager to capture his distinguished bald head and his fat cigar on canvas.

However, this flattering feeling soon fled, for as Oscar perused the paintings, his stomach wrenched. The images were not real likenesses and not at all complimentary. They were ugly and absurd and looked nothing like the real Orr's. Oscar feared that some might find them insulting, especially his sister, Eugenia. He shud-dered to think what she might do when she saw herself with an orange antennae stuck in a greasy black bun.

"I thought ye were one of the modern-like painters who made shapes and colors and things like that?"

"I was. I was one of them," Poppy stammered with wonder-ment. "I haven't painted humans or cars or dogs or houses since I was a little boy. I've painted things that did not resemble real things at all. But I couldn't get you and Miss Orr out of my head, and once I got started, this whole setting became a fantasy to me."

"I can see that," Oscar admitted, riveting his attention on the hubcap flying out of his right ear.

"Shall we call Miss Orr to see the work?" By now Poppy could hardly contain his excitement.

"I'll go find her," Oscar proposed, thinking it best to warn his sister first.

There wasn't far to go, for Ivy and Eugenia were still puttering around the dining room, rearranging the cocktail forks and draping a swag of chintz across the French doors.

"He's done it," Oscar said ominously.

"Done what, brother? What are ye talking about?"

"He's hung the paintings."

"Of course, he's done it. He has been doing it all morning. But good, I am glad it's done." Miss Orr's soprano voice headed for a high note, and Dice covered his ears with his front paws. "Are they beautiful?"

Poppy himself interrupted, "No, Miss Orr, I wouldn't call them beautiful."

"Good," Eugenia said. "With few exceptions, I hate pretty paintings. Right, Oscar? What we call pretty art today wasn't thought so pretty when it was first presented. We forget that. I always say that most pretty art is put on earth so that people won't have to think. Isn't that right, Oscar?"

"That is true," Oscar admitted with relief. "Ye do say that."

"So these paintings are not very pretty. Are they shocking then?"

"Perhaps shocking to some, sister," Oscar tried to caution her.

"When I went on the stage, I tried to rattle my audience's cages, didn't I, brother? They called me 'shocking' on more than one occasion. I didn't want anyone to go away thinking simple thoughts about a pretty voice. The composers didn't want that either. I stepped onto the stage to enter the souls of my audience. Sometimes it was frightening. It scared them and me, too."

"Sister, these paintings are a bit scary," Oscar replied timidly.

"Good. Are they expressive, Mister Poppy? Is that what I'll find around the corner?"

"Miss Orr, the only thing I can truly say is that I painted the only pictures I possibly could."

"Excellent. I look forward to admiring them." With those words Miss Orr hobbled from the dining room.

Oscar steadied his feet and prepared to run to avoid the impact of Eugenia's high, loud scream.

But instead of shrieks of horror and disgust, Oscar heard his sister laughing as if she would burst. "Mister Poppy, these are magnificent paintings!" She squealed. "Mister Poppy, this is art!"

Poppy was greatly relieved. He had not meant any harm, but as he tried to apologize, Miss Orr cut him off. "This is true expression,

Mister Poppy. When I look at these paintings, I am forced to think. I am made to feel. I like that, Mister Poppy. I hope others will regard them as I do."

The reception for the paintings was scheduled to begin at two o'clock. For the occasion Miss Orr had bought Ivy a brand new dress and shoes from a department store downtown. The green floral print fitted Ivy to the waist, flaring into a full skirt with an underslip, accented with new white stockings and black patent leather shoes topped with velvet bows. Miss Orr selected a long blue crepe and a strand of opera-length pearls. Oscar sported an elegant Scotch plaid jacket, navy slacks, with a matching plaid tam-o'-shanter to cover his head. Dice had a floppy purple ribbon tied to his collar. Poppy disliked dressing in anything except overalls, but Ivy said that he should wear something normal. Miss Orr said it didn't matter what Poppy wore because he was the artist and people expected him to look different.

For an hour attire made no difference. Not one person arrived between two and three o'clock, and although Signora Quartuccio and her two young cousins came out of the kitchen to admire Mister Poppy's paintings, their presence did little to reduce everyone's general embarrassment and grave disappointment.

"Perhaps we should eat a little," Signora Quartuccio suggested. "The company is good, the food is good, the paintings are good, so we should eat, no?"

"Yes," the two cousins chimed.

"And drink, no?"

"Yes," the cousins echoed.

"What did I tell you, Signorina Bly? That life is nothing without food, yes?"

"No, signora, you told me that life is nothing without music."

"That is true too, no?"

The cousins, of course, said, "Yes."

As if it were a gala reception for hundreds, a dignified Eugenia Orr led Oscar, Poppy, Ivy, the signora, and cousins, followed by Dice, pursued by cats, into the dining room to fill their pink porcelain plates with authentic Milanese delicacies.

When the front bell rang a little past three, everyone jumped with surprise. Someone had actually arrived. Poppy's eyes lowered humbly toward his plate. Signora Quartuccio hurried her cousins back into the kitchen. Dice, of course, barked at the intrusion.

"Very fashionable people are always very fashionably late," Miss Orr pronounced the words like a natural law. "We'll receive," she declared, and with her brother, arm in arm, they hurried to the entryway.

On its threshold stood an older woman, wrapped in an expensive tweed coat that had long ago gone out of style. She wore mismatched leather gloves and a wide-brim black Spanish felt hat that tied under the chin like a Gaucho.

"Oh my!" Miss Orr exclaimed, impressed by the hat.

The woman before them said nothing. Instead, she waltzed past the Orr's into the hall where she deposited an overstuffed shopping bag onto the marble floor.

"I'm tired," she finally muttered.

"And I am Eugenia Orr," the old lady uttered in return.

"I figured you for her and the big one for your brother. I heard about you."

"Yes?" Oscar queried. "I hope they were good things."

"Couldn't be bad, seeing as how you took to Poppy and Ivy."

"So ye must be a friend of theirs?" Eugenia's voice sang. "We are so glad ye have come. Now if ye don't mind, may I ask ye name?"

"That's quaint. Nobody ever asked me if I minded whether they asked my name. Sure, I am a friend of theirs. We knew each other at the hole they call the *BUENA VISTA CENTER FOR THE UNFORTUNATE*. Unfortunate is correct if you have to go there."

The woman removed her coat and handed it to Oscar, as if he were the butler. The hat, however, remained on her head.

"And ye are who?"

"Me?" The woman pointed to herself. "I am Clarisse."

"Nice to meet ye, Clarisse," Oscar and Eugenia were both relieved to say. "May we take ye hat?"

"No, a hat always stays on my head, even when I'm sleeping. You see I am an old-fashioned woman who was brought up to believe a lady always wears a hat."

"Quite so," Eugenia nodded in agreement. "It suits ye and matches ye dress."

Clarisse smiled with pride, smoothing the pleats on her red print dress. She had found it only yesterday in a donation box of free clothes and was pleased that it had already proven a success.

The tap of Ivy's patent leather shoes and Dice's four paws was heard racing in the hall.

"Aunt Clarisse," Ivy squealed with delight.

"Ivy Bly," Clarisse squealed back. "Look at you, gussied up like an old-fashioned tintype."

"We didn't know ye had living relatives living here," Oscar declared with surprise. "We didn't know ye had an aunt."

"I'm nobody's aunt, but the children at the shelter call me that," Clarisse leaned over Ivy and gave her a second hug.

"It is good to see you, Aunt Clarisse."

"Good to see you too, Ivy. You've grown taller and prettier, and I bet, smarter too."

"I wonder if ye would like a glass of champagne," Oscar suggested, remembering his hosting duties.

Clarisse smacked her lips and whispered to Ivy, "Aren't they a fancy pair?"

Ivy laughed, for despite the large house, Eugenia's collection of rings, the silver, the furnishings, the crystal, and Oscar's Cadillac, she had never thought of the Orr's as fancy. It didn't seem that they cared much about things at all.

"They're putting on their airs today," Ivy whispered back, "because they think it will help Poppy sell his paintings."

"Where in the world is that Poppy of yours?" Clarisse asked. "I didn't walk all the way here with my life in a bag to see a bunch of paintings? I came to see the both of you."

"Poppy, Poppy, Clarisse is here!" Ivy called down the hall.

There was no answer.

"Poppy!" Ivy and Clarisse shouted together.

"Mister Poppy! O! O! O! Mister Poppy!" Miss Orr sang, and above their heads the crystal chandelier tinkled in response.

"I'll bring Mister Poppy back when I get ye champagne," Oscar assured them.

So while Oscar and Dice made their way to the dining room, Eugenia Orr and Ivy led Clarisse to view the paintings.

Chapter 26

" I CANNOT FIND HIM ANYWHERE," OSCAR SAID, HOLDING A TRAY OF
long-stemmed champagne glasses and a bottle of vintage 1956
French champagne.

"What do ye mean?" Eugenia snapped.

"Vanished," Oscar repeated, twirling a smelly Havana in the air like a wand. "Absolutely disappeared."

"That is nonsense and rubbish, brother."

"I looked in the rubbish area, but he is not there. Nor in the dining area. Neither in the hall. Signora Quartuccio said after the door bell rang, he ran into the kitchen, out the back porch, through the gate at the end of the yard, and disappeared into the woods."

"Poppy gone?" Ivy cried.

"Gone," Oscar confirmed.

"Into the woods?" Miss Orr digested the news. "Why on earth would the man want to run away on his big occasion?"

Miss Orr's forehead puzzled for an explanation. It was bad luck about the weather, and so far no good had come of it. Lavish food and drink had been set out for a horde, but no one except Clarisse had arrived to taste it. Now the artist himself had abandoned them. The event certainly had the markings of a total disaster.

Thank goodness, Miss Orr thought, she was a veteran performer. In her decades on the stage, she had faced many unpleasant surprises. Curtains had dropped on her, lights turned off the wrong moment, lines sung out of turn. She had handled failures, international crises, disruptions, natural disasters, and even heart attacks and childbirth in the front row.

"Poppy is a shy man," Ivy said gently, bewildered herself as to why he would take off.

"Very shy," Clarisse concurred.

"Well," Miss Orr shrilled with annoyance, "when the other guests do come, we shall not excuse him by saying he is a shy man. We shall not say he has been struck with stage fright. We shall fib a little and say that the artist has been attacked by influenza and taken to his bed. We shall not mention that he has run away into the woods. Is that understood?"

"Excellent, sister, excellent," Oscar said, blowing a ring of cigar smoke up to the ceiling.

Ivy thought that excuses and fibs would hardly be necessary. She did not believe that anyone else would bother to come.

"Perhaps when they do come," Eugenia continued, "their pity

for his sickly condition will move their pocketbooks in the direction of a purchase." Suddenly cheerful again, she added, "This may be good luck after all."

The minutes ticked by, and then Dice began to bark. From where Ivy stood between the drapes and French doors, she could see a black sedan, as old and as large as Oscar's, moving slowly around the curves of the driveway and heading towards *Tosca*. It stopped in the bend of the horseshoe, and a decrepit old chauffeur slowly opened his door and then in turn opened the two back doors. Three well-dressed young ladies scampered out, followed by a handsome tall teenage boy, in turn followed by an obese elderly woman who held a cane in one hand and a miniature poodle in the other.

Dora Fritz and Eugenia Orr greeted each other in a singing duet. "La, la, la, la, la, la, la, la" went on for several minutes.

Dice and Mrs. Fritz's poodle were less compatible. They greeted each other with growls, and the poodle was scooped up by the chauffeur and confined to the car.

"I've brought my great-grandchildren," Mrs. Fritz declared, making the proper introductions.

The girls and the handsome teenage boy tromped off with Ivy and Dice to explore the table of Italian delicacies. Laughter soon rang through the halls, as the entire back of the house bubbled into life.

Dora Fritz's arrival was swiftly followed by others. Cars filled the driveway and spilled onto the street. Friends of the Orr's, critics, art connoisseurs, collectors, and painting students crowded the house. Foyer and living room were filled with chatter, chairs cluttered with coats and purses, plates stuffed with food, glasses overflowed with champagne. People drank, ate, and discussed Samuel Bly's paintings. Some even took to familiarly calling him Mister Poppy, following Miss Orr's lead.

The weather remained cold and foggy all day. Thick grey mist enveloped the trees and covered the lawn, but guests continued to arrive until all the downstairs rooms were crammed with strange and curious people.

Occasionally, Ivy reappeared from playing with her new companions to let Miss Orr lead her around, "This is Mister Poppy's only child. Let me introduce ye to his daughter, Ivy. She is a girl as talented as her father," Miss Orr rattled on. "No, I am afraid ye cannot meet the father today. The poor man, he has taken to his bed with influenza."

Ivy was in full blush from all the attention. She didn't hate her hair, her birthmark, or her life. Instead, she carried herself with pride, for everyone thought highly of Poppy's work. They said he was a great painter and regretted that he had come down with the flu. Several writers planned to review the show. A gallery owner from New York expressed interest in a solo Bly exhibit. Some hoped they might make an appointment to meet him another day or have him to dinner as soon as he was well. Others said they couldn't live without a Samuel Bly in their collection and commented that the prices were very reasonable.

Ivy, Oscar, and Eugenia beamed, and Dice behaved himself amid all the commotion.

In the late afternoon the twilight mist and noisy chatter were abruptly interrupted by a police car roaring towards *Tosca*. Its red light swirled through the fog, its siren deafened the crowd. Scores of guests pressed against the row of French doors to watch a uniformed policewoman leap across the yard. It was Sergeant Betty Harmon, terribly apologetic to be late.

"Everyone is late," Miss Orr reassured her. "No one is early."

Sergeant Harmon was happily led around by Ivy while cliques and crowds resumed their conversations, their eating, and their scrutiny of Mr. Bly's art.

"May I have ye attention?" The soprano sang out, clinking the side of her champagne glass with the tines of her silver fork. "I would like to introduce ye all to Sergeant Harmon."

The roots of Betty's black hair reddened with embarrassment, as Miss Orr shouted at the top of her highly capable lungs. "We are all here today because of Sergeant Harmon."

The policewoman froze.

"Yes, there she is," Eugenia pointed at the sergeant's shrinking body. "Ye see, if Sergeant Harmon had not met Ivy Bly after she and Mister Poppy were picked up on the highway and had not taken her to dinner at the signora's PREGO, we might have never gotten them back. Indeed, Mister Poppy might have never painted these masterpieces."

Few in the audience could follow Miss Orr's compressed account of the last few months' events, but all understood its implications.

"Bravo!" The cheers went up. "To Sergeant Harmon!" The champagne glasses clinked on her behalf.

Finally, the guests started to go home. A few left with less money and more paintings to add to their collections. Some retired with artistic images in their minds, while others were tipsy with champagne. After several pleasurable hours romping through the rooms of *Tosca*, the young Fritz girls and the handsome teenage boy promised to return to play with Ivy. Before the festivities ended, Dora Fritz and Eugenia Orr had sung several operatic duets. Oscar Orr had smoked six cigars and recited a long poem by the Scottish poet of poets, Robert Burns. Signora Quartuccio's authentic Milanese cooking had been consumed with thorough appreciation, and she now had several new catering engagements. The event had come off as an unqualified success.

There was only one other surprise to report about that memorable Sunday afternoon. It was a telegram that arrived for Samuel Bly promptly at six o'clock and waited importantly for his return under a glass paperweight on the table in the hall.

Every time Ivy passed the light manilla envelope, she tried to feel out its hidden message as if it were braille. She begged the Orr's to let her open it, but of course, they said, "No, no, no!"

It was late when Poppy did return. He was admonished for deserting them but then promptly forgiven for his excruciating shyness. He roared with amusement at the notion that he was suddenly an "important artist," and he sat shocked with delight to find himself a few thousand dollars richer than he had been that morning.

"That means we can find our own place and get out of your hair," Poppy said.

"Ye might want to get yeself out of our hair, but as I said to ye at the beginning of our friendship, Mister Poppy, this house can hold a few more bodies besides the brother and me."

Poppy's voice expanded with gratitude, "I want to thank you for all your help."

"Yes, Mister Poppy, and we want to thank ye for all ye help, too."

Ivy listened with consternation. "Are we leaving already?"

"No," Poppy, Oscar, and Eugenia said in unison, and Dice let out his saddest howl.

"But ye have yeself some choices now, and that's not a bad thing, child."

"Well said," Poppy agreed. "We have ourselves some choices."

"Since money doesn't buy health or luck or brains," Oscar offered philosophically, "as far as I can tell, a few choices are the only thing it is good for."

"Like a new car, brother," Miss Orr chided.

"Don't ye start in, sister, when the old one is running like a top."

It was nearly midnight, and time for bed. Dice was the first to curl up on his rug in the hall. Poppy supported Ivy under his arm and dragged her up the stairs. It was only when they reached the second-floor landing that the sleepy girl remembered the mysterious envelope.

"Poppy, a telegram came for you." Ivy pointed to the bottom of the staircase. "It's there."

Poppy looked down at the marble table, the paperweight, and the telegram with dread. Only bad news arrived in a telegram.

"When did that come?" He asked cautiously.

"A few hours ago," Ivy replied.

"Mister Poppy," Miss Orr emerged from her bedroom. A velvet robe wrapped her tall, frail frame, and her dark dyed hair hung down her back in a thin, stiff braid. "I was putting myself into bed when I remembered ye received a Western Union earlier this evening."

"Thank you, Miss Orr. Ivy just told me."

Poppy peeked into the cellophane window of the telegram. Through it showed the name, Mr. Samuel Bly, and *Tosca's* address. The return address read Saint Luke's Hospital, New York City.

"Open it, Poppy! See who sent it!"

Poppy was baffled. Since they had lost their home, there had been no place to have mail forwarded. He could not imagine who would know his whereabouts in San Francisco.

"Yes," Eugenia encouraged, "it might be good news."

"I have had as much good news as a man with my constitution can take in one day." Poppy rested his hand heavily at the edge of the table. "I'll wait until tomorrow to read this."

"Tomorrow?" Ivy groaned. How could anyone stand to wait to open a telegram?

"Good night to ye, Mister Poppy," Eugenia Orr waved.

"Good night, Miss Orr, and thanks again."

Poppy took the telegram and tucked it into his pocket. He was worn out from the strain of the excitement and much too tired to face any news.

"Tonight, please," Ivy whined above him.

"To bed this minute," Poppy ordered in a tone Ivy dared neither question nor contradict.

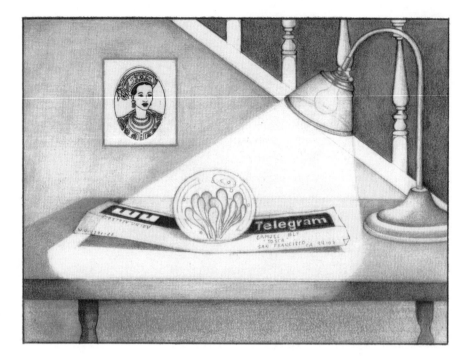

Chapter 27

I VY UNZIPPED HER BEAUTIFUL DRESS, REMOVED HER BLACK PATENT leather shoes, slid off her underslip and white stockings, and crawled into bed. She listened for her father's footsteps or the crinkling sound of a telegram being opened, but as she squeezed her eyes shut to concentrate, there was nothing except the heavy silence of night. Soon she was adrift in that silence, falling, falling, falling asleep.

Downstairs, Poppy surveyed his paintings. With the piano and sofas pressed into its corners, the large living room resembled a museum. Through the French doors the dark grey fog had vanished, and a star winked over the large palm at the end of the drive. Poppy lit one small lamp and took a seat in the middle of the empty Persian carpet.

His hand shook as he slowly lifted the sealed flap of the telegram. Its message was spelled out in teletyped capital letters:

DEAR SAMUEL, CONGRATULATIONS ON YOUR ARTISTIC SUCCESS! I'VE BEEN ROTTEN ALL THESE YEARS, AND NOW THE ROT IS KILLING ME. MY LAST AND ONLY WISH IS THAT YOU CAN FORGIVE ME AND BRING IVY TO MY SIDE. AIR-LINE TICKETS TO FOLLOW. YOURS, FATHER.

Surely, someone must be playing a joke. Those words could have never been written by the man Poppy knew as father. Mr. Bly had lived without regrets, "lived," he said himself, "without having to apologize to anyone." Was it possible that he now begged forgiveness and had a sudden interest in his only grandchild? It made no sense.

Poppy held the paper up to the light. It looked legitimate, but the words themselves belied that possibility. It must be a trick, for never in a thousand years would his father reach out when for so long, he had made a point of rejecting him.

Then Poppy reconsidered. Perhaps the old stinker was really on his deathbed. Perhaps his age and illness had softened him. Perhaps he was in terrible pain and for the first time thought of the suffering of others. Perhaps he was so scared of death he had converted into a loving, parental father. Those were legitimate possibilities. Perhaps.

Poppy's eye wandered down to his father's final request. BRING IVY TO MY SIDE, he read over and over.

Poppy was astonished again. When Ivy was born, he had notified her grandfather, hoping that the presence of a future generation of Bly's might have stirred his interest. There had been a telegram then, too. It read —

CHILDREN ARE OVER-RATED.

There were several other occasions when Poppy had tried to contact his father. Those had met with no response. Poppy might as well have been an orphan, and long ago he had stopped believing it would ever change. Finally, he had stopped caring.

"Ivy!" Poppy exclaimed aloud. Suddenly, it was a matter that could no longer wait until morning.

Poppy bounded up the fifteen steps of the circular staircase to Ivy's room. The stars twinkled on the black glass of her window, and Poppy noted tenderly how she had laid her new dress carefully on the armchair in the corner.

He sat down at the edge of the bed and watched his daughter's composed and peaceful face. He touched the birthmark with his thumb and removed the strands of hair that strayed from her pillow to her mouth.

"Ivy, wake up," he whispered.

The girl peeled back her eyes and looked at her father with wide amazement. Instantly, she shut them again.

"Ivy," Poppy cried urgently, "wake up now."

Ivy rose up in the bed, shaking with alarm.

"The telegram!" Poppy said sheepishly, for now it seemed ridiculous to trouble her in the middle of the night.

"You opened it?" Ivy yawned.

"Ivy, did you do something?"

"Do something?" She repeated with sleepy confusion.

"When you addressed the invitations to the art showing, did you send out any that I didn't know about?"

Ivy's head collapsed back on the pillow and her thoughts drifted into the darkness like bubbles of air. "Maybe," she admitted.

"Like whom?" Poppy asked firmly. "Whom did you send to?"

"I don't really remember." Ivy lifted her arms and threw them around her father's neck.

"Ivy," Poppy said, spilling angrily over the syllables of her entire name. "Ivy Elizabeth Katherine Bly, you do remember. Now tell me whom you sent invitations to?"

"Mother's sister in Australia. Did you know I sent her one?"

"Yes, of course, because you got the address from me. Now who else?"

"Mother's sister in New Zealand."

"Yes, I know about that one, too. Any others?"

"Our cousins in New Mexico."

"But is there anyone else you want to tell me about?" Poppy prompted.

"You haven't told me who sent the telegram."

"Your grandfather sent it," Poppy's voice spiraled like a tornado, "because you sent him an invitation to the art show. Right?"

Ivy pulled a pillow over her head, but Poppy yanked it off and threw it across the room.

"Am I right? Or am I wrong?"

"Right," Ivy's voice was so low that even she couldn't hear it.

"Ivy Elizabeth Katherine Bly, you didn't?"

"I did," Ivy lamented. "Has something awful happened?"

"I don't know," Poppy stammered, for he wasn't yet sure if his father's communication was a good or bad thing. Right now, it just seemed crazy. "Did you write anything when you sent the invitation?"

Shivers ran through Ivy's body. "I wrote a little bitty note, too," she confessed.

"And?"

"That's all," she said with finality, hoping it was the end of their discussion.

"Ivy, what did the note say?"

"I told him that you were a wonderful father and that you had taken care of me without my mother. You had taken great care of me without much money or sometimes even work. I told him that I wasn't an easy girl, that I could be stubborn and mean. Then I said that I loved you and he should try to love you, too."

"Is that really what you wrote?" Tears welled in Poppy's eyes. "Is that really what you believe?"

"Of course, Poppy." Ivy hugged her father tightly. "It's the truth."

"I wish you had told me."

"You would have never let me write to him. Now has something awful happened?"

"Your grandfather is sick, and he wants me to bring you to him."

"Can you?" Ivy asked eagerly. "Can we go to him?"

"Perhaps," Poppy wavered. "We'll talk about it in the morning."

Ivy fell back into a sound repose, and Poppy retired to his own bedroom. For several hours, he tossed and turned, deliberating what to do. By the time he fell asleep, the stars had been replaced by a violet dawn, and Poppy was still uncertain.

The morning appeared brilliant and blue. The customary summer fog remained far out at sea. A warm haze filled *Tosca's* rooms. Birds sang in the trees, and Dice and the cats dozed lazily in the back yard.

"Are we almost ready to go?" Eugenia's voice rippled through the kitchen.

"Go?" Poppy stretched his arms above his sleepy head. "Go where?"

"Mister Poppy, I thought that we would celebrate your grand success with a drive to Mount Shasta." Miss Orr said, busily packing a picnic basket with the leftovers from Signora Quartuccio's feast.

"The car is purring like a tiger," Oscar added.

"Today?" Poppy scratched his head. "Today I must make a big family decision."

"Ye aren't deciding to move out already, are ye?" Miss Orr asked with alarm.

"No, not that."

"Good, then what is it?"

"My grandfather is ill," Ivy explained.

"Was it he who sent the telegram?" Miss Orr's brow wrinkled with concern.

"I haven't seen my father in many years." Poppy's voice choked. "You see, we don't get along so well."

"Perhaps there will be a chance to mend things."

"But Ivy prompted him to get in touch with us without my permission. I'm not sure it's the best thing."

Miss Orr crossed her sharp grey eyes at Ivy. "The girl has a mind of her own, and that is a very good thing."

"Not always," Poppy protested. "In this case, I can't be sure."

"My grandfather says that he will send us airline tickets," Ivy gurgled with excitement.

"Then perhaps ye need to stay here today, Mister Poppy," Miss Orr sighed with disappointment. "Although after ye show, I was sure ye would want to go up to this Mount Shasta."

"Are you certain you want to go today?" Poppy asked.

"Mister Poppy, I don't have much time left to do anything. If I don't go today, I may not be able to go tomorrow," Miss Orr entreated.

"True, sister, neither of us is getting younger."

"Poppy's not getting younger either," Ivy added.

"My brother Oscar will drive, and Mister Poppy can relax in the backseat. Is it far to Mount Shasta, Mister Poppy?"

"Several hours," he answered.

"Then we shall have our dinner there," Eugenia suggested. "We can come back tomorrow in time for a decision about ye father. Perhaps the mountain will help ye make it."

"It is a beautiful day for a drive," Poppy admitted, warming to the thought of dinner at sunset on Mount Shasta.

"That's what sister and I thought, too. We figured it would be good for us to take an outing on such a lovely day."

Chapter 28

THE OLD BLUE CADILLAC AMBLED MAJESTICALLY UP THE highway, heading north and east of San Francisco towards Mount Shasta. Dice and Ivy garbled their own language in the backseat while Poppy dozed and snored. Both Oscar and Eugenia Orr concentrated fiercely on the brother's driving. He held the wheel while his sister told him what to do. Her advice came in warnings, such as, "Watch the truck, brother!" or "Look out for the tree!"

"They're on the other side of the road, sister."

"They may be now, but ye never know what a thing is going to do."

Near Sacramento they left the cool ocean breezes of San Francisco behind them. A relentless hot wind from the valley blew through the open windows of the car. It blew hotter and hotter and hotter, so that the four humans dripped with perspiration, and the dog panted heavily with his tongue.

By the time Oscar pulled over for a picnic lunch, the heat had affected everyone. Poppy awoke from his nap in a grouchy mood. Ivy said she had a stomach ache and didn't want to eat. Anxious Oscar thought the Cadillac might overheat if they had to climb any hills. Eugenia commented that this journey might be her last. Dice refused to get out of the car.

"It's bad luck that Mount Shasta is so far," Oscar lit a fat cigar, took a tiny puff, and extinguished its stubby end. "It's too hot to smoke, too."

"Bad luck, good luck," Miss Orr said tiresomely. "When will every little thing ye do stop being a question of luck?"

"That happens to be my world view," Oscar pouted.

"We know, brother, we know. We are quite aware of ye world view."

Grumbling loudly, Oscar fetched the picnic basket from the trunk of the car and dropped it with a thud on top of the roadside table.

"No one feels like eating, brother. The child is sick, and Dice is so hot he can't move. It's so hot ye can't even smoke one of ye cigars."

"Let's eat," Poppy spoke up. "In fact after we eat, we'll all feel better."

Poppy prepared a paper plate for everyone, heaped with ravioli, gnocchi, cannolli, and Quartuccio-baked buns.

Ivy protested, but Poppy persuaded her to nibble. Spirits rose with food and cold drinks, and by three o'clock the group had resumed their journey north. This time Poppy took over the task of driving, and their rate of travel improved considerably. Less than two hours had elapsed before Mount Shasta's gigantic dome loomed before them on the horizon.

"Oh, Mister Poppy!" Eugenia Orr sang the words with thorough approval.

The peak rose like a grand expression of royalty, a sovereign queen gowned in immaculate snow, surrounded by her subjects — forests, rivers, fields, and lakes.

Poppy pointed to a path through a withered summer meadow, up over purplish volcanic rock. The sun had started its dip on the west side of the mountain, and the snowy robes glittered like white gold. "Now we'll have a little walk."

"Mister Poppy, brother and I will rest here in the car." Eugenia declared, "You see we are quite old."

The Orr's were quite old, Ivy thought. They were old indeed. Poppy was not so old, but he was getting older. She was getting older, too. Her mother had died young and would never grow old. Her grandfather must have been born mean and old, but now he was sick and wished he were young.

Poppy walked some distance ahead, and Dice tugged on Ivy's sock, coaxing her to hurry along.

"Wait for us," Ivy shouted.

Poppy shaded his eyes with his hand, watching Ivy bounce up the hill toward him. His daughter's thick hair flew back like a pony's mane, and her face was radiant. A great relief swept through him, for his daughter looked not only healthy and well-fed but well-loved, too. It was not only Poppy who loved her, but Dice, the Orr's, Aunt Clarisse, Sergeant Harmon, and Signora Quartuccio. They all appreciated Ivy. Poppy thought how lucky she was to have their love and wished her grandfather, old Mr. Bly, had given her his love, too.

Poppy touched the top of Ivy's head and turned back towards the mountain. Dice and the girl followed, trying to keep pace. The path ascended to a field of boulders. From there they viewed the broad valleys south and the mountain ranges, whose dark edges were outlined many miles to the west. Ivy felt swept up like a bird, suspended over a landscape that unrolled forever. Each time Ivy came to the mountain, it felt as if she were re-meeting her mother. Today the three obsidian rocks rested snugly in the pocket by her leg. She slipped her hand over their cool smoothness. As long as she lived, Ivy knew that she could return to Mount Shasta and her mother would be there, in the dust, air, and snow, waiting for her.

That would never change.

"What are you thinking?" Poppy asked.

Ivy's thoughts had turned to dreamy pictures inspired by the colors and shapes of the scenery below.

"Thinking?" Ivy mused. "I was thinking about mother and Grandfather Bly."

"Your grandfather?" Poppy voiced his surprise.

"You should give him to a tree. Miss Orr's mother taught her that when a great sadness comes into your life, you can give it to a tree."

"Then what?" Poppy was skeptical.

"I'm not sure," Ivy admitted reluctantly.

"So why would I do it?"

"Miss Orr said that afterward you don't have to hold it by yourself anymore. The tree keeps it for you, and whenever it hurts, you can hug the tree."

"A poetic idea," Poppy agreed.

"No, Poppy, it is a real idea. Miss Orr has filled every tree at *Tosca* with her heartaches. Did you know her first husband was the most handsome man in Spain?"

Poppy looked over the vista of the landscape and felt like Ivy, airborne and suspended. "The most handsome in all of Spain is very handsome indeed."

"Yes, but he died of yellow fever, and she was broken-hearted." Ivy sat down on the tabletop of a large purple boulder. She scanned the nearly treeless slopes until she spied a grove of scrub juniper some distance to the east.

"I couldn't remember the trees on Mount Shasta so that's why I gave mine to the palm at *Tosca*. It is the prettiest tree in the yard, don't you think, and it's the tallest too so it's closest to the sky." Ivy gently patted her heart. "I think it helped."

"I'm glad, princess. I'm glad it helped."

Now Ivy took the lead up the path toward the junipers.

"That's why I thought you might want to do it, too." Ivy prompted, "Go on."

"Sometimes you have to be very young for special things like that to work." Poppy looked deeply into his daughter's eyes.

"Sometimes they only work if you are young."

"Miss Orr isn't young," Ivy objected. "Her brother isn't young."

"But I don't believe that you can lose a part of yourself by talking to a tree." Poppy broke off a juniper needle, inhaling its crisp conifer fragrance. "Maybe it works if you truly believe it."

"I didn't believe it," Ivy kicked the rough ground with her shoe. "I didn't believe it a bit, but I wasn't afraid to do it."

"So you tried it." Poppy admired a disbeliever who would try anyway. That was the sign of a curious mind.

"Try it, Poppy." Ivy insisted. "Try giving grandfather Bly to that tree."

Poppy looked around with embarrassment.

"Go on," Ivy urged.

"I couldn't, princess. It's too silly for me."

Ivy turned back down the mountain, away from the summit of the dazzling peak. She and Dice retraced their steps along the rocky path. When she turned around to look for Poppy, at first she couldn't see him. Then tucked behind one of the junipers, she spied his arm flung around a tree. Maybe, she thought, it will make a difference.

"What a naughty wee dog ye are," Miss Orr exclaimed. "Ye cannot let an old lady rest for a minute."

Dice wagged his tail in agreement, barking, licking, and jumping from Oscar's lap to Eugenia's.

The sun set slowly on the snow cone of Mount Shasta. The white cap glowed in layers of pink, red, and magenta before turning violet and grey. Its dark shadow towered above them, luminous and eternal.

The quaint old lodge where they spent the night was a place Poppy had once stayed with Ivy's mother. Its lobby was filled with musty furniture and a large stone fireplace spanned an entire wall. Redwood timbers crisscrossed the ceiling, and round hook rugs covered the floors. There were cases of books and an untuned, upright piano in the dining hall. Upstairs the mattresses sagged from the weight of a century of visitors, and basins with pitchers of cold water served as sinks. Each of them slept like babies under the white eye of Mount Shasta.

The next morning the powder-blue Cadillac once again rumbled its way along the highways of California. The great mountain disappeared behind them. The forests thinned to suburbs. The glistening city of San Francisco stretched out along its great bay.

"We're home," Ivy thought. "San Francisco is our home. This is where we belong."

On *Tosca's* doorstep was a packet. There were two airline tickets to the East, and marked in block letters at the top of each one were their names, SAMUEL BLY and IVY BLY. Also included was a short hand-written note, scrawled in an old man's shaky script.

COME SOON.

Poppy examined the tickets and studied the simple note.

"Will we go?" Ivy searched her father's face for the answer.

"Yes, princess," Poppy sighed. "We'll go soon."

"Will it be all right?"

"It will be whatever it has to be." Poppy took his daughter's hand and pressed it to his lips, "Maybe there's a chance that we can make it better."

THE END

Summer Brenner was raised in Georgia and migrated west, first to New Mexico, then to Northern California. She has published seven books of fiction and poetry, including *Dancers and the Dance* and *One Minute Movies*. She is currently working on a new collection of stories.